HALO ROBERTS

Finding My One

This novel is entirely a work of fiction. The names, characters and incidents portrayed in it are the work of the author's imagination. Any resemblance to actual persons, living or dead, events or localities is entirely coincidental.

Halo Roberts has no responsibility for the persistence or accuracy of URLs for external or third-party Internet Websites referred to in this publication and does not guarantee that any content on such Websites is, or will remain, accurate or appropriate.

Second edition

ISBN: 978-1-7770505-7-3

Advisor: Terri Stepek
Cover art by Teshia Saunders

This book was professionally typeset on Reedsy.
Find out more at reedsy.com

For the readers who wanted to know the rest of Veronica's story...
sometimes you just need a little country...you know...balance.

"One is the loneliest number that you'll ever do…"

-THREE DOG NIGHT

Contents

Rude Awakening

*S*trong hands cup my jaw, tilting my face up as his lips claim mine. Grazing my lower lip with his teeth he sucks it in to bite it lightly as his hands slide into my hair. Gathering up a handful, he kisses his way along my jaw and pulls my head back, just rough enough that I gasp and then sigh with pleasure.

His other hand slides down my arm to my waist, finds the hem of my shirt and lifts it up, tickling my belly as his hot fingers find my skin. Releasing my hair he uses both hands to push my shirt up, but before I can raise my arms to help, he flips it over my head and then uses one hand to pull it tight at my back, pinning my arms.

I'm panting with need, tits about to burst from the lacy bra that's now on full display. Eyes drinking me in, he palms one, thumb teasing the nipple that's about to drill a hole in the bra. Sliding his hand up to the strap, he slides first one, then the other off my shoulders, never letting up the pressure that has my arms pinned to my sides.

Sitting down on the couch, he pulls me closer, his face nuzzling between my tits as one hand slides under my skirt, cupping my ass. I moan *BEEP* and sigh. *BEEP*. His *BEEP* mouth is *BEEP* hot and *BEEP* wet and *BEEP* I struggle *BEEP* wanting to *BEEP*. SON-OF-A-FUCKING-ALARM! DAMNIT! *I can't even get laid in my sleep...doesn't matter, this is not a dry spell, this is a CHOICE. Why would I need a man? I'm rich, I'm young, I'm beautiful, I am having the time of my life.* My tingling clit is not fooled...it would very much like a man to take care of it right now.

Grumbling I fumble for my phone and dismiss the alarm, hoping if I shut my eyes fast enough, my dream man will be waiting. No such fucking luck. With a sigh I sit up, toss my sleeping mask off and get out of bed. Crossing the room I throw open the heavy curtains to let the morning sun wake me up completely.

Stretching I head into the studio adjoining my bedroom, tuning into a podcast to catch up with last night's gossip as I flow through my yoga poses. An hour later I'm feeling centered as I shower and ring for breakfast to be brought to my suite. I have no desire to eat with my father this morning. I'll deal with *him* later.

Pause for Effect

V eronica

"I do not care! Kidney stones? That's horrifying, why would you share that information with me, I don't need to hear that!" I grab the edge of the desk, leaning closer, making sure my point is clear. "Do you know what I _do_ need to hear? I need to hear who was in charge of my security detail when I missed Claire Saint James' Red Party. It happened _yesterday_ and I missed it because my guard had _kidney stones_ and _shockingly_ there was no alternate!"

I pause to let the full effect of my astonishment and dismay sink in, no tantrum works if you don't pause for effect. My father is sitting at his desk, not looking at me, I follow his line of sight and glance over my shoulder. The drinks cabinet...figures. He always has looked for a way to hide from his problems. I challenge him at every turn and not once has he ever just stood up to me. I plan to keep pushing until he does, it's my favorite

3

game.

"Tell me, *Father*, how exactly does that happen? How exactly do I have *one security guard*? Why is there not a fucking platoon of them waiting their turn to protect me? YOU are the one who insists that I have these fucking babysitters. Do you understand that just because he had to leave, to go to the damn hospital, my driver refused to take me and wouldn't let me go with anyone else without my guard?!"

Pausing again, mostly because I need to breathe, I open my mouth, preparing to launch into another diatribe.

"Enough." At the sound of her voice, my blood runs ice cold and I swing around, goosebumps speckling my skin.

"Mother," I can't keep the surprise and a tinge of fear out of that one word. "What are you doing here?"

Tough Love Sucks

*V*eronica

Stiletto heels clicking on the polished wood, Evelyn Rockford strides across the study and pours brandy into two tumblers. Crossing the room, she hands one to my father with a small smile, and then turns to me, leaning back to sit on the edge of his desk. She takes a sip of the brandy, looking at me carefully over the rim of the glass.

Her hair is dark, glossy brown like mine, she has a shot of silver right at the part of hers, and it's rolled up in a twist, not a hair out of place. Dove grey suit with a pencil skirt, white blouse, all tailored to fit her slim body perfectly. Pearls at her neck and ears. The picture of steely success. I come by my ice princess persona through genetics, *and it works on everyone but the woman who gave it to me.*

Silent in this mini battle of wills, I maintain eye contact, pulling the fragments of my cool back around me and settling my nerves. I get what I want, when I want in this world. I raise my chin, carefully keeping my hands in place, refusing to be nervous. *I wish I believed my own bullshit, god I need to pee.*

"I scheduled a break in the lecture circuit to come home," Evelyn says coolly, setting the glass on the desk with a clink and crossing her arms, "because your father and I want to make some changes." We continue our stare-down as my mind races, I don't want anything to change, I like things just the way they are, *my way.*

"You're spoiled Veronica. You always have been and, I know, it's our own monster we've created," she holds up a hand to stop me as my mouth drops open in outrage, *monster?!* "We've always wanted the best for you, and we know that we've been very busy…perhaps too busy to notice that you've become an adult with no appreciation for anything." *Well this is bad, where is she going with this?*

"Why didn't you have a backup guard last night you ask? Because they refuse the job! It's not as if you're in any actual danger of attack, they are mainly there to protect you from making a *fool* of yourself, and the last three companies we've engaged have given back our retainer fee. Most recently because, and I quote, 'that spoiled brat needs a spanking not a babysitter'!" Smoothing her skirt with her hands as she regains control, Evelyn avoids my eyes. Reaching for her glass, my mother takes another sip and then swirls the brandy, her eyes on it, contemplating her next words.

"The Oceanics line is going over like a dream," Evelyn says brightly, "and the market is screaming for more organics. We want to introduce a line of cottons that supplement all the skin care and makeup products, and I'm bringing you in at ground zero." She pauses and glances at me, and I'm thrown off. I don't know what to say, I can't even decide if this is good or bad news.

My parents were born into money, and when they got married, they built an empire of skin care products used exclusively in high end day spas that cater to cruise ship clientele. My mother is the spokeswoman for the brand, she was a model for a haute couture fashion house in Paris when she met my father. He was in a position to get her face time with key players at a time when cosmetic regenerations cruises were the next greatest binge of the wealthy.

Even now, in her late 50s, Evelyn could easily pass for a woman in her 30s. She has perfect skin, rigorously protected from the sun, and she is her own best client of the line that my father's partners developed. Over the years, they've expanded, and cornered the market in organics, another favorite buzzword of the spa set. *Let's only put this shit on our faces if it came from nature with a 600% markup, people are fucking sheep.* My mother is currently on a lecture circuit, bringing new physicians and aestheticians on board, expanding the line.

My sole job since attending university; where I was queen of my sorority and managed to secure a degree in marketing, *in spite of myself and the little weed habit I tried out along the way;* was to be a socialite, maintain my social media presence, and spend Daddy's money. I carefully developed this job for myself, having vigorously resisted my father's early attempts to bring me into the business.

My mother had always been good about leaving me alone, I would occasionally attend seminars with the uber-important clients, assisting mostly by allowing my mother to claim my skin was the result of her Oceanics line. *Joke's on them, I almost never remember to use it, I sleep in my makeup, I just have great skin.* I give her Oceanics line a plug and a hashtag once in a while, and we all live happily ever after. *I thought.*

"I think you'll have to define, 'ground zero' before I decide if I'm interested, Mother." I'm careful to keep my tone cool and respectful, a tiny bit of suspicion coloring my words.

"I think *you'll* have to decide if you enjoy your allowance Veronica," Evelyn counters quickly, voice rising slightly, "you are 29 years old. We are no longer interested in footing the bill for an aging socialite who refuses to use her brains and talent for anything other than spending money she didn't earn!"

AGING? My head explodes, and I gasp loudly in outrage.

"We want you to be happy, darling," my father says quietly. *Well that's fucking hilarious, you want me to be happy? Don't tell me I'm aging at 29.*

"Your father and I just see you going through the motions, attending parties, spending money, but where are your friends? Where is the experience? What memories will you have when you truly are old and grey?" My mother smiles, looking straight into my soul, her blue eyes going stormy grey with emotion.

"We love you darling, and after that little fiasco with Nick," *ugh, do not mention Nick, that one hurt, he was the first man who wasn't just taking me on a test drive because I'm rich and gorgeous, he was good...and we didn't work because of me.* "We just don't want you to become sad and irrelevant," she murmurs, unaware that she has just surgically removed my heart, set it on my father's desk, and lit it on fire.

My eyes narrowing, I spear her with a glance, sharing it with my father who is now watching me instead of his glass of booze. I have no words, my parents are assholes. Turning on my heel, I storm out of the study, catching the door and shoving it shut behind me with a resounding boom. I hear my parent's voices before the door slams but I ignore them, moving quickly up the grand staircase and down a long hall to my wing of the house. Shutting the doors to my suite, I sit at my makeup table, breathing heavily as I stare at my reflection in the mirror.

'Sad and irrelevant'? Well I don't look happy, I'll give them that. My dark brown eyes are glittering with anger and unshed tears. What my mother doesn't understand is that she just casually threw out my greatest fears. I know I haven't done anything with my life. I don't know what I *want* to do, I *hate* being alone.

Although if I'm honest I know it's my own fault. After a few attempts to make friends in high school and college, only to realize that they were looking straight at my trust fund, I stopped trying. Shallow relationships with people who have as much money as I do is all I've been able to manage lately, drinks, parties, shopping, the occasional fling. *My mother is right, I fucking hate it when she's right.*

Leaving all the insulting old-maid commentary out, I think back about the conversation in the study. I'm intrigued by a cotton organics line, and I find myself wondering what she meant by 'ground zero'. But I'll be damned if I'm going to go ask now, no way, not showing this weak underbelly to the shark that is my mother. It can wait until dinner.

When my mother is home, dinner is a formal affair. We eat in the dining room, there are courses involved, and we dress for dinner. I decide to put my best face forward, I refuse to show hurt feelings when I've decided I want to hear what she has to say. I pull a silk sheath in royal blue out of my closet and get ready for dinner as if I'm preparing for battle.

Banished Before Dessert

*V*eronica

My parents are conversing quietly when I enter the dining room, my father spots me first, and I watch the emotions play across his face as I walk to my place at the table and sit. I know I've never been fair to him.

My mother told me once a long time ago about the day he lost his sister. She had a rare disease, it wasn't his fault, but he was young too and he always felt incredibly guilty for surviving. Having his own daughter brought that all back for him, and it's always been very easy to get him to give me anything I want. *It's official. I'm a brat.*

Catching my father's eye, I give him a tiny smile and begin eating. I'll let my mother start the conversation. She doesn't disappoint.

"Looking at our conversation earlier, I could probably have been less… harsh," Evelyn pauses without looking at me, taking a sip of wine. She tosses a glance at my father and he nods encouragingly. Meeting my eyes, her gaze softens.

"Veevee we love you," *oh for the love of Pete she's pulling out Veevee, that is low, even for her.* "We want you to work with us, we want our family to be strong and united. We want you to enjoy your life, but at the same time we want you to find something you love, something of substance, something that will last when the parties are over." Evelyn sighs, taking another drink, watching me.

"Tell me about the cotton line," I decide to skip the part where I tell her she's right. Her eyes brighten, she didn't want to slog through the emotional stuff either.

"I've been in contact with a farmer that is using 4th generation organic seed," she begins excitedly, "we really want to keep it exclusive, made in America, highest quality, worthy of tying to our line." I nod and keep eating as she continues.

"What we need, and what we feel you would be perfect for, is to start the marketing operation right in the fields. Our clientele are particularly impressed with products that have strong ties to the land. They want things to come straight from the farm, no factory or production line involved." She's talking faster now, warming to the topic. "Of course we can't get away from some of those production aspects, but that's where we want you, finding ways to show our buyers the quality and hard work that bring them the cotton organics." She pauses again, watching me closely, giving me time to respond.

"Okay, so to be clear," I pause, trying to order my thoughts. "Are you saying you want me to visit this farm?"

"Oh not just visit," my father breaks in, "stay as long as you need...to be able to...sell the entire experience..." he tapers off lamely, catching the furious head shake my mother is giving him. She sighs and turns to me again.

"Well that's not how I would have told you, but yes, we'd like you to move into the community for a time, immerse, find all the selling points, really bring that straight from the cotton field aspect to our clients," my mother concludes firmly.

"You want me to move to a town." *Shudder.*

"Yes, Tara will handle the details."

"You want me to spend time on a farm." *Shudder.*

"Yes."

"Where exactly is this farm that I have to *move*? Why can't I just go visit it a couple of times?" I watch my parents exchange a glance and I can tell this is the part they're not sure they can slide past me.

"Northern Georgia," my mother says quietly, "in an adorable town called Gravity-"

"Geor-you just said adorable town, oh my god how many people are we talking, are we still at least over 100,000? Tell me this is a big enough place that I will not go insane. Tell me." I cut in, eyes darting between my parents, having flashbacks of the summer camps I was sent to from the time I was ten until they asked my parents to stop sending me. *Yeah, good times.*

"Enough," my mother's voice cuts through my little trip down memory lane. "You are no longer going to just live the party life, you are part of our family and you will be part of our business," her voice is rising, and I'm sensing the hammer is about to drop. "You are going to Georgia," she turns and nods to one of the staff, "We're ready for dessert." *And just like that, the party is over and I'm moving across the fucking country. But let's have dessert. Sure. Why not.*

Well This Is... Quaint

*V*eronica

Landing in the third, *third* airport required to fly to my new ...*temporary* ...home, I'm digging in my bag for sunglasses to fight off the Georgia sun as I walk across the tarmac and enter the slightly cooler interior of the terminal. The airport consists of one terminal and three gates. I am in hell. Looking around with a sigh, I locate the baggage claim, which is more of a fenced in pen holding my two large bags. I'll have more things sent when I know what I need. *Or if I'm even staying...if I can handle this place.* I head for the exit, looking around for the driver who should be waiting for my arrival.

I almost miss him, I just happen to read the piece of paper he's holding up to his chest that says 'Rockford'. The man is in a denim shirt, jeans and dusty boots. He looks to be in his 50s, his face tan and creased with lines, obviously he spends his life outdoors and in the sun. I pause and turn, walking back to him, and he smiles.

"You Veronica Rockford?"

"Yes, that's me," I respond, completely out of my element.

"I figured, there weren't too many options," he laughs, holding out a hand, "I'm Carl, I work on the farm, Shane sent me to get you." I take his hand and shake it briefly, it's warm and covered with callouses. His easy smile and folksy manner are calming my nerves. He easily lifts my bags and leads the way to the exit.

Leaving the building, Carl gives me a hand up into his truck, it starts with a roar and we're on the highway. Carl tells me we have about 30 minutes of driving ahead of us, and then he falls silent, occasionally offering little bits of information. We reach town and he points out the main shopping area, *yikes,* there's a movie theater, a few restaurants, a few more bars, several churches. I feel like I'm on the set of a movie about a small town, I have never been anywhere this tiny. Gravity, Georgia, population: 7,437 *plus one.*

Carl stops the truck at a small complex a couple blocks off the main square. It's quaint, all the units have their own entrance, townhouse-style like little cottages, *I'm pretty sure my first doll house was bigger.* He stops in front of the third one in the row. A small sidewalk leads to a tiny porch, the trim is white and the siding is grey and the window boxes are full of red and yellow flowers. Carl hops out of the truck, coming around to give me a hand down before getting my luggage out of the back. Walking me up the sidewalk he turns a key in the lock and then hands it to me and opens the door.

"Home sweet home," Carl smiles, waving me through the entrance. He doesn't come in, just stands in the doorway for a minute while I look around.

"The lady working for your dad, Tara? She said they should

be bringing you a car tomorrow," Carl continues, "She had a few groceries delivered and furniture, towels, sheets and all the kitchen stuff got put in earlier this week, so you should be alright for tonight." He runs a hand through thinning blonde hair, then jams his hat back on his head.

"Yes, everything looks fine," I look around, still getting my bearings, *my personal maid has larger living quarters.*

"Should I drive the car to the farm tomorrow?" I turn back to find Carl watching me with interest, like I'm some kind of zoo animal.

"Naw, I don't know what time they'll bring it, I'll just swing by and get you after breakfast and chores. Shane wants to give you a tour, figure out what you need from us and stuff like that, so I'll see you around nine." He waves and heads out the door before I have time to reply.

Giving myself the grand tour doesn't take long, from the entry, stairs lead up to the second floor which has an adequate master bedroom with a bathroom, and a second, smaller bedroom that will most likely be my office or yoga space. The main floor is all open in a circle around the stairs, to the right is a small dining area which leads back to a kitchen, to the left is a large living room. A back door leads to a small fenced in yard with two chairs and a table on a cobblestone patio. Just off the kitchen is a small laundry, *yeah right,* and a door to the single garage that sits off the back of each unit dividing the yards.

Everything looks new at least, Tara obviously played to my style as much as she was able, the living room and kitchen colors are neutrals with splashes of blues and greens, high quality furnishings tastefully arranged throughout. The woodwork and trim is white and clean. The bedding and towels are luxurious with a high thread count. *I don't know what I expected but I suppose this will do.*

Checking the refrigerator, I find a bottle of white chilling, some cheese and a small loaf of bread. Perfect, I hate cooking. Slicing some cheese onto a plate, I add a hunk of bread and open the wine. Grabbing a wine glass from the cabinet, I fill it and head for the backyard. My first dinner in Gravity.

Leaning back in the chair, I'm amazed at how many stars I can see. The night is so clear, not a cloud, *no city lights or smog.* Now that the stress of planning for this trip and actually getting here are over, I'm starting to stress about the next leg of this forced adventure.

I've spent so much time staying under my mother's radar, doing only what I needed to do to make sure my allowance kept appearing in my account. A little voice in the back of my mind wonders if that was all time wasted, maybe I should have done more, *obviously.* Maybe if I had, she wouldn't have felt like she had to force me into this new venture. I go back over the last few times we've spoken, wondering where I made the mistake that got her attention.

I wonder about the farm. I know nothing of agriculture, at all, zilch. Heading back to the kitchen I drop off my dishes and grab my laptop, setting up on the couch with the rest of the bottle of wine. What's done is done, the important thing now is proving that I can succeed. Failing this job, *and seeing the look of smug disappointment on Evelyn's face that would be sure to follow,* is not an option that I am able to tolerate.

Three hours later, I feel like I know more than is going to be necessary about cotton production and the area in general. I'm starting to believe that marketing the sheer wholesomeness of this place is going to be simple. I haven't emptied the bottle, so I head back to the kitchen and put it away. Glancing at the counter, the dishes are still sitting there, dirty. *Oh...right.*

I dig around and find dish soap and a sponge. No sense in figuring out the dishwasher for three dishes. As I scrub, rinse and lay them on a towel to dry, I see something in the backyard. Drying off my hands I cross to the door and flip on the outside light. I worry it might be an animal, maybe a raccoon or something, but there's no way in hell I'm opening this door to go check. As my eyes search the darkness just beyond the pool of light, I see a kitten nosing around the ground under the chair I was sitting in, scrounging for crumbs.

I've never had a pet before, and I refuse to count the horses my father has purchased in my name over the years. I didn't even get to ride them, they were racers. With a gasp I throw open the back door intending to scoop the kitten up and snuggle it close. I'm an idiot. The kitten races out of the yard with a hiss, diving up and over the fence, little claws scrabbling, and disappears.

With a rueful laugh, I head back inside, turning off lights and locking the doors, and I realize this is the first time I've ever done these things for myself. Grabbing my phone off the counter, I stare at it for a moment. No notifications. I mean, of course, my social media is going strong, but not one text. None of my friends asking me how I'm settling in, or asking me out for drinks because they didn't realize I left today, nothing.

Okay, so now I'm having a moment. Not one of those bitches care if I'm gone? Can't check in? Can't tell me I'm already missed? *None of them miss me, why would they? All of my 'friends' only truly love themselves...* Blowing out a sigh, I stare at the text strings on my phone for a long minute.

With a little thrill buzzing up my spine, I delete them all. I'll keep the contacts, it would be stupid to get rid of everything, but I've had a revelation. For the next month, *or three or six or however long I have to be here*, I'm essentially off the grid to the people back home. It will be my own little social experiment to see who makes contact. Feeling resolved, I walk up the stairs, shower and fall into bed, ready to tackle whatever the farm has to offer tomorrow.

Country Meets City

Shane

As Carl's muddy truck bumps up the lane, I catch my first glimpse of his passenger. It's hard to tell what she looks like, her face is half covered by a huge pair of sunglasses, and her hair is dark. He stops the truck and hops out, giving me a wave as he heads around to open her door. Taking his hand to gingerly slide down out of the truck, she turns and brings out this huge ridiculous woven sun hat and covers up shiny brown hair with it, then she grabs a big purse and steps aside letting Carl shut her door.

It's been three months since Evelyn Rockford's people contacted me. I even had one conversation with Evelyn herself, and there hasn't been a day since that I don't wonder if getting into business with them was a bad idea. I dedicated some land to organics a while back, and this is really what I was going for, until she told me that my local contact would be her daughter.

Veronica Rockford…I generally don't bother with computers unless it's for business, and I shouldn't have bothered this time, but I did a quick search. As photos of celebrity events, tabloids articles, *and selfie after selfie on every social media I've ever heard of and about a dozen that I haven't* scrolled across the screen, I felt a moment of panic. Then I spent the last two months wondering how in the hell I'm going to babysit this spoiled socialite from the city and still get all my work done.

I find myself already annoyed with her as she takes her time, fiddling with her stupid hat and the strap on her purse. *This is a mistake.* Ignoring me completely, she turns in a full circle, using one red-nail tipped hand to lower her glasses for a better look around. With a little sniff, she puts the sunglasses back in place and teeters around the truck following Carl, who has his face averted to hide a smile. *Great, this is going to be just great.*

Taking my time, I put down my tools and wipe my hands on a rag as they approach. I know her name is Veronica, I hope she has a nickname or something, but she doesn't really look like a 'Vicki'. She's wearing a yellow blouse with the sleeves rolled up part way, tied in a knot at her waist. She's got on a denim mini-skirt, just long enough to avoid a scandal, and five miles of smooth tan legs end with, I look twice, just to be sure, high heels. *Ho-ly shit, what the hell am I gonna do with a princess?*

Yanking my eyes up to meet hers before she catches me staring at her legs, I hide a smile because I'm pretty sure that because her skirt is made of denim, she dressed in her version of 'farm'. She walks delicately across the dusty gravel drive with Carl, I wipe my hands again and step around the tractor to meet them. She holds out a hand, and I take it carefully, her hand is delicate but strong, she smiles politely.

"Shane Tyler, glad to meet you." I squeeze gently and release her hand, nervous. Maybe I was supposed to clean up, I'm doubting pretty much everything about this venture except for the money they're throwing at me at this point.

"Veronica Rockford, thank you for taking the time to meet with me, I know you must be…busy," she says coolly, glancing around again. With her face hidden behind those big sunglasses, I can't gauge her, but the little pause while she came up with 'busy' pisses me off. I'm no longer interested in taking Her Majesty on a tour.

"I sure am *busy*, this is a working farm, Carl will take you on a tour out to see the cotton fields. Carl, I guess you'll have to take the gator instead of the 4-wheelers and skip the east farm today." My voice is too harsh so I shut up and flick a glance at Veronica's legs before I turn and walk away, grabbing a couple of tools and heading to the back of the tractor I'm working on.

Carl knew I was planning to be the tour guide, but he recovers quickly and starts chatting away, pointing out different buildings as he leads Veronica to the shed where the gator is parked. A few minutes later they roar off down the lane, she's using one hand to hold the 'oh shit' handle and the other to hold on to her stupid hat. *Damn she's beautiful…too bad she doesn't belong here.*

Accidental Peep Show

*V*eronica

    I keep a smile on my face as Carl chats away, letting my sunglasses hide my eyes and the fact that inside I'm fuming. Meeting Shane Tyler did not go well, and I'm not even sure where things went wrong. It seems like taking the 'gator', which turns out to be a golf cart on steroids, is an insult, but I don't know why. *I also don't know what the hell a 4-wheeler is, the gator has four wheels...or maybe six...farms are stupid.*

Shane Tyler. I was surprised he wasn't older, I was expecting someone more like Carl, but Shane had to be in his mid-30s. He's tall, broad shoulders, narrow hips and when he walked around that tractor and shook my hand, the visual sent a rush of heat straight south. Too bad that dark blonde hair and those brown eyes were attached to an asshole.

Carl gives me a quick tour of the building site, he says this isn't the main farm, just a place where they store and work on the big equipment so it doesn't all have to be at the home farm. He points out some pieces of equipment that I recognize from my research last night, and then we head out on a small gravel road.

I'm enjoying his easy southern drawl and he isn't expecting me to contribute much to the conversation, which is a relief. Slowing down, he rounds a curve in the road and we come to a small bridge. Just before the bridge we turn and head into the fields. He drives about 100 more yards and stops, getting out of the gator.

"Well, I figured this would be a good place," he says, watching for my reaction. Pulling off my sunglasses, I turn in a slow circle. This place is beautiful. Fluffy white tufts attached to dark stems as far as the eye can see. The bridge leads over a small river that borders the field, it rushes merrily over the rocks. Across the river there are more cotton fields and further down there's a large white farmhouse, its lawn butting up to the fields at each side, separated by a slat rail fence. The house is facing the river, and several buildings are spread out behind it including a huge barn, all painted red. If I Googled farm, a picture of this place would pop right up.

"From a marketing standpoint, this is going to be a breeze," I laugh, walking over to stand by Carl in front of the gator. He takes me over to the edge of the field, showing me the plants, picking me some stems in a tiny bouquet. He lets me wander a bit as he leans on the hood of the gator. After I've seen my fill, we head back up the road, and I point out the house.

"That's the Tyler family farm," Carl says, "we're going there next, lunch will be ready soon." *Great. I'm not sure I want to see Shane again right now, I spent two minutes with the man and he appears to despise me.*

"I see," I turn and narrow my eyes at Carl, "so…why did we have to take the gator instead of the 4-wheelers?" Carl chuckles, slowing the gator and turning between a couple of outbuildings, he slows even more behind one of them and points out a smaller machine that looks like a motorcycle on four wheels.

"That there is a 4-wheeler, so you can see it's not going to work if you're planning to wear clothes like that out here," he waves a hand vaguely at my skirt and heels. "He figured you'd each ride one, I guess he thought maybe you'd be a little… sturdier." *Oh. Well, fuck.* I blush a little, luckily my sunglasses hide most of my face.

"Understood, I'll wear something smarter tomorrow." *Also there is no fucking way I can drive one of those things. Sturdier? These people are crazy.* We pull up near the house, and Carl hops out, stopping at the water pump near the garage to get a drink as I look around.

It's a great big farmhouse with a 2-story wrap around porch on two sides, the upper porch is screened in, the bottom is open. A big old dog is sleeping on the porch in the sun, he lifts his head as we walk up, thumping his tail briefly before going back to sleep.

"Worthless mutt, that's Barney," Carl mutters fondly, scratching the dogs ears before leading me around the side of the house. Another covered porch, this one much more utilitarian, houses an outdoor sink and shower, racks for muddy farm gear, and shelves with several piles of jeans and t-shirts neatly folded. Carl kicks off his boots and after a moment of confusion, I place my heels beside them, and we head into the house. This side entrance leads to a laundry with a bathroom attached, walking through, there is a staircase disappearing up and a doorway leading to the kitchen.

"Judy? We're here, I'm sending Veronica in," Carl hollers, waving me through as he heads back to the laundry to 'get cleaned up'. I walk into the kitchen and a small woman with light brown hair shot through with grey appears, bustling around as she cooks enough food to feed an army. Her eyes twinkle as she smiles at me.

"You must be Veronica, I'm Carl's wife, Judy. Come in, come in, sit," she waves me to a chair at the big farm table and hands me a glass of sweet tea, then continues to whirl around the kitchen. Recognizing that I am seriously out of my depth, I don't offer to help, instead accepting the tea and watching her cook.

We make a little small-talk, she asks how I like it here, *I don't,* how my trip was, *ridiculously inconvenient,* if I'm finding the farm interesting, *not even a little.* I give her the easy, correct answers, *yes, great, very,* and ask her a few questions, finding out that she and Carl live in a smaller farmhouse just up the road a half mile. Carl joins us, getting himself a glass of tea and giving Judy a squeeze and a kiss before sitting at the table. His fresh-scrubbed face makes me aware of the dust on my own and I excuse myself.

Heading back through the laundry room to the attached bath, I find a washcloth and towel and wash my face and hands. The water feels so good, I quickly strip my shirt off and wash my neck, chest and arms as well. Toweling off, I shake my shirt out and movement to my right catches my attention.

I didn't pay attention, and the small window over the toilet is wide open. Shane must have been walking by on his way into the house. Right as I look, his eyes meet mine. His are so *very* dark. His jaw twitches as if he is grinding his teeth and he quickly walks out of sight, entering the house loudly and

25

heading for the kitchen. *Oh my god, this day just gets better and better.*

I quickly pull on my shirt, finger comb my hair, and square my shoulders before marching back to the kitchen. This simple farmer is not going to get the best of me, I am Veronica Rockford, I always get my way! I will do the job and go back to civilization! *Damn that man for being gorgeous.*

"Judy, can I help get anything to the table?" Chin lifted, I avoid his eyes, Judy smiles and hands me a heaping bowl of mashed potatoes. Together we get all the food on the table and in that few minutes, several more hired men appear, taking what must be their usual seats. Ranging in age from a young kid with white-blonde hair that looks freshly out of high school up to another man about Carl's age, it's a good natured, rowdy bunch. I can tell they've been strictly instructed, probably by Judy who mothers them all impartially, to be on their best behavior.

I can see now why Judy made so much food as these men pile their plates high and demolish second and third helpings. I'm full to bursting after one plate, *I'm going to need to watch it, wouldn't that be just perfect if I've gained 15 pounds the next time I see Mother.* I can't pass up the pie though, Judy dishes up warm peach pie with homemade whipped cream, and I'm pretty sure I've died with the first bite.

"That's why you hear of Georgia peaches, honey," Judy laughs, enjoying my reaction, giving me a pat on the shoulder. Pushing back from the table, the men begin to take their dishes to the counter, thanking Judy and heading back outside. Shane gets up too, he's been quiet most of lunch, pushing in his chair he sets his dishes on the counter and turns to head outside. He stops in front of me, and I stare at him coolly as I watch the internal struggle unfold.

"Carl show you around?" He finally mutters, glancing at me and then down at his hands.

"Yes, the fields are beautiful," I'm not sure what else to say. He nods and starts for the door again, only to turn and come back.

"I was rude earlier, I'm sorry," he says gruffly, "I found something in the yard on my way in that you might like. Do you want to see?" His dark eyes meet mine and he gives me a panty-melting grin. Not trusting myself to speak, I nod, getting up and putting my dishes on the counter before I turn to follow Shane outside.

New Name, New Deal

Shane

I lead Veronica out the side porch and across the yard, past the garden to a spot near the roots of the largest oak tree. Looking carefully, I find the little pile of grass I saw earlier and motion her close. Carefully lifting the shredded grass I smile as I hear her give a quiet little gasp as she sees what is underneath. A small nest of brown baby rabbits, huddled close together, little dark eyes blinking at the light. Veronica's hand trembles as she reaches out a slim finger to stroke one between the ears.

"Do you want to hold one?" I look at her and her eyes are bright, a rich chocolate brown with amber flecks. She shakes her head slightly and strokes the tiny ears again.

"No, thank you, I don't want to scare them. They're so tiny," she breathes, "I've never seen them as babies before, they're beautiful." Staring at them for a few more moments, she finally reaches out and takes the grass from my hand, her cool fingers brushing mine, and carefully replaces the grass over the babies.

She stands, brushing invisible grass off her skirt. Before I think about what I'm doing, I reach out and gently take a piece of grass out of her hair and then tuck the lock of hair behind her ear. Her eyes meet mine and the air between us feels charged with electricity. I find myself taking a step toward her when I hear a familiar rumble on the road. Startled, I try to smile and act normal, *was I just about to fucking lean in? Like I'm going to kiss her? It's been so long since I've looked at a woman that I'm ready to grab the first one that shows up?*

To be fair, she's the most beautiful woman to ever set foot on this farm, but a quick glance down at those heels is a reminder that she doesn't belong here. This is nothing but a job she can't wait to be done with so she can get back to her city life.

"Katie's bus," I say hurriedly, waiting for her to begin walking with me, "My daughter." Her eyes widen, but she nods, keeping pace with me as we cross the yard. Veronica sees Katie get off the bus and start walking up the lane and glances at me, confused.

"You must have become a father pretty young," she says carefully. Usually I would blow this off with a 'yeah'. I don't know why I give her the quick version before Katie is in earshot.

"My older sister, Heather, was killed in a car accident ten years ago, Katie was her daughter. Heather's worthless husband didn't want to be a dad anymore without Heather around. They were pretty young when they had her, so he signed his rights over to me the day of the funeral and I adopted her," my voice is low, remembering that scared little girl who cried herself to sleep in my arms every night for months.

"She was seven when Heather died. I was 23, not ready to be

a dad, but we've figured it out together." My chest is warm, I love that kid walking up the lane as if she were my own.

"She's 17 now, and all the girly-stuff scares the crap out of me, but we get along. My folks are retired and live in Florida most of the year, so Katie spends summers and spring breaks with them. Carl and Judy have kind of stepped in as another set of grandparents, that's been a huge help." Veronica is quiet, taking it all in as Katie bounces up to us, smiling.

"Hey Dad, I got the lead!" She bubbles, I reach out and crush her to me, planting a kiss on top of her curls.

"Great news kid!" I turn us towards Veronica, who is watching us. I'm wishing I hadn't told her anything, I don't want her to bring it up with Katie, and I sure as fuck don't want sympathy. Glancing at her, I'm relieved to see the same cool expression on her face, not a trace at all that she might feel bad for Katie, or for me.

"Katie this is Veronica, she's the lady from the city that's working with us on the organic thing." I'm watching Veronica's face, realizing I'm simplifying everything.

"Nica," Veronica pronounces it Knee-cah, and she smiles holding out a hand for Katie to shake. Katie looks terribly impressed, with good reason. Even after spending the day bumping around a dusty farm, Ve-…Nica, *I'll have to get used to that…*looks like the wealthy socialite she is, beautiful and polished.

"Veronica is so stuffy, if I'm going to be here a while we can take down the formal a few notches, agreed?" Nica smiles at both of us, then turns to Katie, "So, the lead? School play?" Katie nods enthusiastically, telling Nica all about the tryouts as they turn and walk to the house. They stand on the porch for a few moments, Katie chattering a mile a minute, before she heads inside. Veronica turns and walks back down the stairs. Pausing for a second while she's still about twenty feet away from me, she seems to be thinking. Giving her hair a little toss, she squares her shoulders and marches over to me again.

"Mr. Tyler…" She pauses, and I interrupt.

"Shane." I don't know if she's getting formal to set the tone or what but that's not going to fly out here. *If one of the hired men ever heard her call me Mr. Tyler…I'd never hear the end of it…*

Her lips tighten and she takes off her ridiculous sunglasses for a moment, looking at me with narrowed eyes. It's an assessing stare, it puts my back up and I'm about to say something that would most likely end this partnership in a hurry when she speaks again.

"Fine. *Shane.* I think that sometimes when I am thrown into a new situation, I can get a little bit…tense." Her chin is lifted as she watches me for a reaction. Other than a little head jerk, I don't react much. I can't even come close to guessing what is rolling through her beautiful head. She sighs heavily, looking away and fiddling with her sunglasses a moment, putting them in some sort of fancy case before jamming them in her purse. I'm not saying a word, I'm more interested in hearing where this is going. She sighs again, looking at me as if she's almost mad I'm not reading her mind. *Sorry darlin', whatever you're thinking, you're just going to have to spit it out.*

"I didn't want to come here." She says it so fast I'm slow to react, just staring at her for a moment.

"What makes you think I'm excited about this situation, Princess?" The words are out before my brain catches up, my shoulders bunch angrily and I'm about to open my mouth to holler at Carl to take her back to town. *I knew this was a bad idea.*

"I KNOW!" She loudly hisses in my face, surprising me, her hands are clenched in fists at her sides. She brings them up to cover her own mouth for a moment, her eyes wide.

"I know." Her voice is calming, her hands lowering again. She takes a deep breath and it hitches on the way out. Taking another one, she meets my eyes.

"I know you don't want me here." Veronica says quietly. "Why would you? It's a burden you obviously don't need, and I can only begin to guess what my mother paid you to be a part of this 'little venture' as she calls it." Veronica's slim fingers add air quotes to 'little venture' as she rolls her eyes. She sighs again, with an angry little head shake.

"This farm, this job, this is all my mother's *grand design* to force me to prove my worth," she continues, her expression fierce. "Please understand, I'm not trying to tell you that I'm special or that I need special treatment, I just want you to know that I jumped out of the plane with no parachute."

I give a small laugh, and she flashes me a sad little smile, fluttering a quick hand as I open my mouth to speak.

"No, please just let me finish." She waits for my nod and takes another steadying breath.

"I've never had to work for a single thing in my life. Not one thing. The money was always there, and it could buy *almost anything.*" Nica stares at me and I stare right back, her brown eyes are hurting, begging me to hear what she can't make herself say. *I wonder what it couldn't buy, that's what she can't tell me... maybe she doesn't even know.*

"All of this has forced me into some long overdue and fairly painful self-reflection. I've lived the 'charmed life' of a spoiled fucking princess...there it is in a nutshell." Her gaze is faraway, and she gives herself a little shake, her eyes meeting mine again.

"I don't know why I thought you should hear all that. Maybe I just needed to say it. The fact is, Evelyn is expecting me to fail," Nica says bitterly, "and I'm going to need your help not to let that happen." Her hands cover her lips as if she's praying and stopping herself from talking anymore at the same time, obviously waiting for me to respond.

"I'm sorry for judging you before I even met you," I start, and her eyes widen a little. "It was probably a bad idea to search you on the internet too…"

"Oh my god…" her surprised gasp and then the blush that stains her cheeks makes me smile.

"I'm not going to fault you for wanting to show your Mama you can stand on your own two feet. Side note, she's scary as all hell, even on the phone." She can't hold back a laugh at that, and I join her, enjoying the moment.

"Look," I bring it back around as she grows quiet with a happier sigh, "me an' you can find a way to work together… maybe you won't hate it here as much as you think."

"I don't hate it, it's beautiful here…in a dusty-roads-sort-of-weird-smell kind of way," her smile tells me she's teasing now. *I think we're both trying to find our way out of our little moment without being awkward.*

"In the spirit of partnership, I promise not to wear high heels to the farm anymore if you will promise to tell me about any other blunders I may be making along the way." Her voice is light, more collected now. "I'll do my best to learn quickly and to stay out of the way."

"Scrap that hat too and it's a deal." I don't know where that came from, but the look on her face is comedic gold. She pulls the hat off her head, the ends of her long shiny hair fluttering in the breeze and then I think she surprises both of us when her head tilts back, her mouth opens and she laughs. A real, honest, straight from the belly laugh, ripples right out of her beautiful mouth, and I can't help but join her. *Maybe this new partnership won't be complete shit after all...*

When the laughter fades, she smiles, eyes sparkling and it's like a weight has been lifted off of us both.

"Fair enough, I'll get a different hat," she says with a saucy salute, turning and heading across to the garage where Carl is tinkering around while he waits to take her back to town. She calls to him and he joins her at his truck, a minute later it roars off down the lane.

Standing there for another moment, I finally shake my head and laugh again, heading to the machine shed to get back to work. *Nica* is certainly full of surprises.

I've Got a New Daydream

*N*ica

So I'm not sure what exactly prompted me to have them call me Nica. Maybe just that feeling of new place, new me, new attitude I felt last night crept in…for whatever reason I don't want Shane and Katie to call me Veronica.

Secretly, I've hated my name since my freshman year of boarding school when the girls in my dormitory nicknamed me "Vero-knickers-in-a-twist". They made up a song about it… with dance moves. One of the few friends I had during those horrible teen years called me Nica. It never stuck, but I always liked the nickname.

Carl pulls up to my little townhouse and I realize I've been silent most of the ride. The conversation I had with Shane was a huge relief. I can't *believe* I spoke so openly about my mother and my fear of failure. He just seemed like a safe place to dump my fears. *Why? I just met him, and everything feels different.*

He's expecting me to be a princess, *he said as much*, and I want to prove him wrong too. *I wish I knew why his opinion of me matters...we just met...he's nobody to me.*

Even in my own mind, it's hard to admit that he's already *not* 'nobody'. Those intelligent brown eyes strip away all of the little barriers I've built to keep myself protected and leave me feeling bare to him. Telling people about your thoughts and feelings and, *shudder,* dreams in my world is like screaming out every weakness you've ever had from the highest mountain. I think things might be different here, *with Shane*.

Hoping Carl doesn't notice the flush running up my neck, I open my door and hop out before he gets out to help me.

"I'm fine, it's been a great day, tell Judy the peach pie was amazing," Carl agrees, smiling. "Also, if you could, just let Shane know I'd like to wander around the home farm a couple more days? Maybe run some marketing ideas by him? I'm going to need to get a camera out there and do a few preliminary photos, maybe some short videos. We need teasers for my mother to present on the upcoming line."

"Will do, and thanks for the short name, it's easier for this old man to remember," Carl nods at the silver SUV he's parked behind, "looks like they dropped off your car, I'll tell him, we'll see you tomorrow." Tipping his hat at me, he laughs quietly, "have a good evening *Nica*."

Heading into the townhouse, I grab a glass of wine and head upstairs to the office. Cell service at the farm is sketchy at best, and I didn't think to ask about WiFi. Now that I have a good signal, my phone is blinking. My parents, checking in *like they give a shit,* Mimsy *took her days to even realize I left town,* and a text...

Shane: Nica suits you, sleep well.

Well, that's just lovely...now I won't sleep at all.

Wandering back downstairs restlessly, I head for the kitchen. The outdoor light is on, and through the back door window, I can see the kitten has returned. Leaving the lights off, I slowly creep up to the door and watch it quietly. At one point I move slightly and it glances my way, so I know it can see me, but it doesn't run away. I watch it for a few more minutes until it jumps up into one of the chairs, settles on the cushion and closes its eyes. I turn off the light, smiling to myself. *That's enough for today.*

Heading upstairs, I turn on the shower. Stripping down, I step into the hot water and let it pour down my back, steam filling the room. Washing my hair, I feel the soap suds running down my body, watch them swirl at my feet and I'm thinking of Shane.

I want it to be his hands on my body. I want those strong hands to pinch my nipples, squeeze my ass, I want to feel all the power in that body driving into mine. I want to hear him yell my name.

Running my hand down my belly I lean against the wall of the shower and start circling my clit, my breath coming faster.

I want to knot my fingers in his hair and wrap my legs around his waist. I want him to slam me against the wall and fuck me hard.

My other hand slides up to pinch and tease my nipple, I'm so close.

I want him to spank my ass pink while he's fucking me, jolting me until I come so hard I forget my own name while I'm screaming his.

My eyes shut tight, I climax, gasping, the water pounding my body. *Shane.*

A Text Goodnight

Shane

Me: Nica suits you, sleep well.

Sitting on the edge of my bed, I hit send and immediately wish I could take it back. What the fuck am I doing? *Day one I'm trying to figure out a way to melt the pants off the ice queen. I'm letting my dick do the thinking and it wants her bad.*

After our breakthrough today, I should keep this business, I should not mix things up with Nica...*Nica, god I want to grab a handful of her hair, pull her head back and kiss her until we're both gasping for air.*

When I saw her standing in the bathroom today, in that tiny denim skirt and her lacy white bra, it was all I could do to walk away from that window. Her tiny waist, willowy figure, generous tits filling her bra. Waterfall of dark hair pouring down her back. I'm rock hard just thinking about her, I lay

38

back on the bed, popping open the fly of my jeans to relieve the pressure.

She's very carefully walled off anything that might make her appear weak, that much is obvious. I can't imagine trying to live in her world, city life seems so much more complicated than it is here in the country. She cracked a little today, when we talked, and even before that, when she saw the baby rabbits, and when I touched her hair. The way her eyes darkened with need when they met mine through the window for that brief moment.

I wanted to shove that skirt up around her waist and bury myself balls deep in her heat. I wanted to watch her nipples harden and her cheeks flush and her tits bounce, I wanted to make that woman come harder than she ever has before with my name on her lips.

Standing up, I push my jeans off my hips and kick them off, boxers too, and head for the shower. *So I can jerk off in there... I'm only fucking human.* Later, when I'm lying in bed and sleep is about to take me, my phone pings.

Nica: good night Shane

I Don't Have A Thing To Wear

N^{ica}

Waking up the next morning, I feel out of sorts. What possessed me to respond to his text? What did he mean Nica suits me? Is that an insult or a compliment? I believe the problem is that I've never met a man like Shane, I'm used to men who are sophisticated and cultured and always complimentary. It bothers me that I'm pretty sure a compliment from Shane would have to be earned. *It bothers me even more that I want his attention...I want it bad.*

Resolving to get back to the business at hand, I force myself to focus on yoga, shower *quickly,* dash off an email to Tara to get the ball rolling on a small crew for the preliminaries, and head for the local mall.

Looking through the clothes I brought with me, it quickly became obvious that very few items were, in fact, practical for wear at the farm. Driving to the only group of stores in town, pointed out by the helpful Carl when I arrived, I wish I was back in the city, at the stores I love. *Not that any of them have 'farm' wear.*

Finding the largest department store, I park and square my shoulders, marching inside. *Woman on a mission, I will not die if I have to wear something off the rack...I will die a little, but not completely, it will be an adventure.* Pausing inside, I let my eyes adjust to the much more fluorescent lighting.

"Can I help you find anything honey?" A pleasant voice inquires, and turning I find the voice is attached to an equally pleasant looking woman, somewhere in her 40s, with curly strawberry-blonde hair and sparkly hazel eyes.

"I believe you could, I'm doing some work at the Tyler farms and I'm going to be outside a lot, marketing crew, I'm sure you understand..." realizing she has no idea what I'm talking about, I taper off lamely, lifting my chin to hide my embarrassment.

"Well hon, I'm not sure what a marketing crew does, but I do know farm clothes," she laughs taking my elbow, "my name is Nancy, let's start with jeans." Over the course of the next two hours, I am introduced to a full-scale farm wardrobe, and my new friend Nancy proves to be witty and full of common sense opinions as I try on all the options.

Finally, tossing the last shirt over the door as I put my own clothing back on, I realize that I'm having fun. Opening the dressing room door, I collapse on the bench outside as Nancy hangs the last pieces back on the rack.

"Well Nica?" Nancy grins, "Find anything you'd like me to ring up?"

"Yes please, that rack will do and I'd like the short boots in both dark brown and tan, and let's add a hat that doesn't make me look ridiculous." I cock an eyebrow at Nancy as her eyes widen and her mouth drops open in a little O, she gives her head a little shake and laughs.

"You got it hon! Need help getting all this out to your car?" She starts pushing the rack towards the front, taking the card out of my hand as she passes.

"My car? Why on earth would I put all these clothes in my car?" I'm confused, unsure how stores operate in small towns.

"Well, how do you usually get things you buy to your house?" Nancy is smiling gently and I'm sure I should probably feel stupid at this point.

"I select the pieces I want and they're wrapped and delivered to my home where my personal maid…puts..them..away…oh." I'm blushing furiously.

"Huh," Nancy clucks her tongue, looking at me, "are you hiring?"

"What?" I'm confused and completely over the novelty of small-town shopping at this point.

"Well hon, it sounds to me like you're all the way out in the boonies by your lonesome and could use someone to help you out." Nancy holds up both hands like she's trying to soothe me as my eyes narrow, "Now, hear me out. It seems to me you could use someone to run errands? Do your shopping? An assistant-like?" She pauses, gauging my reaction, before continuing quickly, "I actually have someone in mind."

Twenty minutes later, Nancy is on her lunch break, and she hops in my car, directing me to a bar about a mile from the shopping area. As we pull into the parking lot, I eye the establishment carefully, unsure how to avoid offense.

"I'm not eating here," I say flatly, deciding honesty is best.

"Oh god honey, neither am I, your new assistant works here." Nancy's eyes become fierce and she stares at me hard. "Her name is Wren, she's 21, and she's saving up to go to nursing school in the fall. Jobs are scarce around here and she's putting up with the shit-head who owns this place swatting her ass and drooling all over her until she can afford to leave."

Glancing through the grimy front window, I see a harried little figure moving quickly around, tray of drinks balanced carefully, dodging as if she's avoiding more than just the owner's hands. I turn off the engine and get out of the car.

"I'll be right back," Nancy nods, wide-eyed, scrambling out of the car to follow me. Pushing the door open, I walk into the restaurant and conversations grind to a halt, curious eyes turn my way and I decide to take full advantage of the attention.

"I'm looking for Wren," I announce, she's disappeared, probably into the kitchen, and sure enough after a moment, her blonde head pops out the door, blue eyes wide and curious. Wiping her hands on her apron she walks quickly over to me as I fold my arms and wait.

"Yes ma'am? I'm Wren." Her voice is musical, very sweet.

I notice a large man pushing away from the bar. He tucks thumbs in his belt loops, bringing his pants dangerously close to falling off of their precarious perch under his sizeable gut. Leaning forward, I speak quietly so that only Wren can hear.

"Wren, Nancy tells me you need a new job, I need you to quickly tell me the name of your employer and then I need you to gather your things and go outside, can you do that?" Her eyes widen and she looks scared and excited at the same time. Glancing over my shoulder, she must see Nancy which gives her the reassurance she needs, because she gives a tiny nod.

"His name is Wayne," she whispers and then turns and quickly walks back through the door to the kitchen, Wayne watching her with beady eyes. When she reappears just a few seconds later, she isn't wearing her apron and she has a small, shabby purse on her shoulder.

"Wren!" Wayne bellows, rendering the restaurant silent, "Get your ass back to work girl! Your break isn't for another hour." He glances at me with a leer, "Unless you've come to apply for her job, sweetheart." Gnawing on the toothpick hanging out of the corner of his mouth, the man repulses me. Wren has frozen, unsure, watching me.

"Go on outside, I need to have a conversation with Wayne," I nod at her regally. Taking full advantage of my five-inch stilettos, I'm as tall as Wayne. She scuttles past before he can block her path, passes me with a grateful glance and is out the door in a flash. Wayne turns to me, angry, I cross my arms and stare him down.

"Wren is no longer your employee, Wayne." I hold up a hand, stopping his words as he begins an angry retort. "If this is going to be an issue, our next conversation will be with the state health inspector present." I pause, letting the threat wiggle into his tiny brain. I run my finger along the edge of a nearby table and glance at it before taking a napkin and carefully wiping it off, a clear expression of disgust on my face.

"I'm guessing the local official has been keeping his eyes on the money you put in his hands, instead of the state of this roach-infested cesspool." I smile sweetly to counter the insult, keeping him off-balance as he gapes like a fish, furious.

"I can see that you're upset, Wayne." I quirk an eyebrow at him as I feel a sardonic smile stretch my lips. "Just believe me when I say my pockets are deeper, my grudges last longer, and if you think I'm a bitch...you don't *ever* want to meet my mother." Turning on my heel, I see Nancy holding the door open, eyes gleaming. I give her a small smile as I stalk through the door and walk across the parking lot.

Before I get in my car, I text my mother's assistant, Tara.

Me: I need you to check into the health and safety records of the Highway Bar-n-Grill in Gravity, make sure it gets a visit from someone other than the usual inspector within the next week or so

Tara: you got it V

Setting Up Shop

Nica

"I'm going to ship these samples to your mother, call the photographer with your notes about that filter, and take care of your shopping today. Is there anything else you want me to work on?" Pen at the ready, earnest blue eyes look at me over a small notebook.

"Thanks, Wren, that will do, check in later please." I smile as she waves and heads out the front door. That girl is amazing. Smart, sweet, conscientious, she completes every job I give her to perfection. If I didn't know she was planning to attend nursing school I'd be figuring out a way to keep her working for me long-term.

I stretch and stand up, looking out the front window. With Wren helping and more team members around periodically, I have reconfigured the dining room into office space. With the help of Tara and overnight shipping, I've added a lot of personal touches. The townhouse is so small it's sort of what I imagine camping would be like, but it's really starting to feel like my own space.

It's been a week since the scene at Wayne's, and everything for the first campaign is coming together smoothly. I've only seen Shane in passing, I haven't exactly been avoiding him, but when I do see him I'm usually with a photographer or the new blogger I'm collaborating with, never alone.

I'm not sure I want to be alone with Shane. Even when I see him out working, those dark eyes burn into me, stripping me bare and sending a shiver of need to my core. That man is a bad idea. I sit back down at the table, trying to get back to work and failing. I'm too distracted, I need to move.

Switching to workout clothes, I lace up my shoes and head out the front door. I let my mind wander, taking in this cute little town as I jog on the sidewalk for a few blocks before reaching a park I drove by the other day situated next to a lake with a biking/running trail. It's a gentle four-mile course and I finish it and continue on past my townhouse again, heading for downtown.

Running around the courthouse and through the town square, I notice several older buildings in a row that are vacant, and one in particular catches my eye. A large sign is being put in the window announcing it's going up for auction one week from today.

I've been feeling claustrophobic in my makeshift office since I brought Wren on board, not to mention needing space to work with other team members every time I bring them to town. The building is on a corner, with a second story window that is curved right around the corner over the entrance. It's unique for the row because it's the only one with a third story.

It has the fancy facing similar to the rest of the buildings, but I can see that the roof is also different as it's pitched rather than flat. The brick and decorative tile seem to be in reasonably good shape, and I'm intrigued by that curved window. Sliding my phone out of my arm band, I snap a picture of the auction poster and head back to my townhouse.

Invigorated after a good run, I kick off my shoes at the door and head for the kitchen, grabbing a bottle of water. Leaning on the counter to stretch, I hear the doorbell chime. I'm curious because I'm not expecting anyone today, but I probably accidentally locked Wren out. Grabbing a towel off the counter, I pat my face and toss it around my neck as I walk to the front door.

I barely contain a gasp of surprise to find Shane standing there, his shoulders filling the space as he leans against the door frame, thumbs hooked in the pockets of his jeans. A curl of dark blonde hair has fallen forward onto his forehead and I resist the urge to brush it back. His dark eyes are hooded and sexy and I'm completely off balance. *Also I'm a sweaty fucking mess, great.*

"Shane! Hi! What's going on?" *NO! Too bubbly, stop it you fool!* "Would you like to come in?" *Better. Now just stop talking.*

"Thanks," he grunts, stepping inside but stopping in the entryway, glancing at his boots.

"Oh no, it's fine, do you want a bottle of water?" He nods and I lead the way to the kitchen, extremely aware of a bead of sweat tickling my skin as it tracks a path between my boobs. I desperately want to make him wait while I go shower and change. I can't help but smile as I hear him pause to kick off his boots and pad along behind me in sock feet.

It's Friday Night

❧

*S*hane

She's wearing these tight little black pants that stop just below her knees and a red tank top over a sports bra. Her dark hair is all pulled up on top of her head in some kind of messy knot, little pieces falling out to stick to her neck. Must have caught her right after a workout. Her ass is fucking perfect with a tiny bounce as she walks into the kitchen.

I stop to kick off my boots and have a stern discussion with my dick at this point. I am simply here to check in, she is working hard on this first round of marketing stuff and I know she's putting in long hours. The grapevine in this town works faster than the internet service starting with Wren and ending with one of my younger guys on the farm, Mike.

Wren. What Nica did for that girl was unexpected. Wren told Mike all about the scene with Wayne, how Nica took him down without him uttering a word. It's easy to think of Nica as a shallow, rich brat who doesn't really belong here. I think everyone keeps wondering when this place is going to be too backwards for her, when she'll just throw in the towel and charter a jet home. After the talk we had, and knowing what she wants to prove, I think she's dealing with it all just fine.

She stays, and she works, and she showed up at the farm the second day she was here in jeans and a cotton blouse and an honest-to-god pair of farm boots. *Looked damn good too.*

Katie thinks Nica is quite possibly the coolest person she's ever met, and Wren practically worships her. All the men like her too, she doesn't boss them around, she asks smart questions, and she tells the crews she brings out to stay the hell out of the way if the men need to get work done. *So why is she avoiding me...and why the hell do I care...*

I walk into the kitchen as she turns from the fridge and sets a bottle of water down on the counter near me. Her eyes are curious and she seems nervous. I want it to be the kind of nervous that means she likes me and is happy to see me, like butterflies and shit, but I don't know if that's what she's feeling. Looking around at the kitchen, I crack open the bottle and take a drink.

"So, how's everything going? You need anything?" *I sound like a dumbass.* "I mean, looks like you've been working long hours," I wave a hand in the direction of her dining room table, piled high with samples of stuff and papers and her laptop. I feel like a fucking idiot at this point, because the truth is I showed up today because I just wanted to see her. Now I'm here, and she's watching me through thick black lashes with those big brown eyes and I realize I should have thought a lot harder about what I want to say.

"Um, yes, everything is going well, I'm having Wren ship a lot of things to my mother that will help as she develops the initial pitch, I don't think I *need* anything exactly." She laughs lightly, taking another drink of water and glancing out the window.

"Good, good, um, that's great." *Fuck. Fuck. Fuck. Award for most awkward conversation ever goes to me.* "So, why are you avoiding me?" *Fucking hell...*I take another drink of my water because I didn't mean to ask her that, and now it's out there. I think I'm just going to go outside and lay in the street until something runs me over because that would be far less painful than this conversation.

"Sorry, I guess I thought you were very busy and I've had Carl helping me and..." her voice is clear and cool, and her eyes are holding mine. I just nod, amazed that she's making me feel *less* stupid. "...well, I didn't want to annoy you, and after I understood the comment about gators versus 4-wheelers, I kind of thought you mostly found me to be an idiot." Nica is blushing but her chin is up, and she's watching me.

"I'm sorry about that," I grumble, uncomfortable again, "public relations was never my specialty." I shrug my shoulders, stuffing my hands in the pockets of my jeans. "Anyway, I was thinking maybe you'd want to take a break, since it's Friday night and all," *her eyes are so pretty.* "There's a sort of festival this weekend, it starts with a street dance tonight, there's food and stuff, the music should be pretty good," I pause, waiting for her to say something. *This was a bad idea.*

"I've never been to a street dance before, or...any kind of outdoor festival really..sounds fun," she says lightly, then laughs deprecatingly. "What does one wear to a street dance? I'd like to avoid looking horribly out of place." She crinkles her nose at me and I speak without thinking.

"Darlin', you look beautiful in everything." The moment the

words leave my mouth I feel stupid, until I see her eyes widen, and glimpse perfect white teeth as her lips part in a tiny, pleased, smile. She takes a small step towards me, I bet she doesn't even know she did. It takes everything in me not to strip off her clothes, set her ass on that white counter and bury my face between her thighs.

"They're uh, pretty casual, I'll pick you up at six," I turn and bolt.

"Ok, see you tonight Shane," a tiny bit of uncertainty tinges her voice as I pull on my boots, I look back once at those gorgeous brown eyes and smile at her. The uncertainty vanishes as she smiles back and I head for my truck. *Ho-ly shit.*

He Called Me Darlin'

*N*ica

I stand at the door long after his truck leaves the curb, a dazed smile stretching my lips. *I think Shane just told me I was beautiful and asked me on a date, and ohmygod I could listen to his Southern drawl say 'Darlin' allllll day long.* Blowing out a sigh, I wrench myself out of a daydream and head upstairs to shower.

Wrapping my hair in a towel and pulling on a shirt and shorts, I force myself to get some work done. I smile as my fingers fly across the keyboard. It wasn't long ago, less than a month, that an invitation to any sort of event would have required a full day of preparation. *Look at me having some priorities, Mother.*

Wren returns and I glance at the clock, I have about two hours before Shane picks me up, *now* it's time to get ready. Wren quickly files away some receipts and turns to look at me.

"Do you need anything else for today?" She's practically

dancing with nervous energy.

"No, thank you, big plans for the weekend Wren? I stand, stretching.

"Oh, just going to be at the Spring Fest, there's a street dance tonight, the band is really good…um, Mike asked me to go with him." Her eyes are sparkling with excitement.

"Well you have fun, maybe I'll see you there, I'm planning to check it out." I smile as her eyes widen with surprise.

"Really? I mean that's great! I didn't know if it would be your thing…" she stutters a little, embarrassed, "um, I mean, not that it's not fun, and not that you…I don't know…um, are you going by yourself? Do you want to come with us?" She is such a sweet girl, *I better check into this Mike.*

"Oh thank you for the offer, but no, I actually have plans to go with Shane, maybe we'll see you there." Wren's mouth drops open in a surprised O.

"Shane Tyler? Wow, like a date? He never comes to these things, all he ever does is work, that's what Mike says anyway," Wren giggles, "he must think you're something special."

"Well, I don't know about that, but I'm sure it'll be fun," I brush off her speculations, "You'd better go on and get ready." Wren giggles her way out the door and I close it behind her with a sigh. I don't want to think too hard about what tonight means. *Because I really like him…and it scares me…*

Heading upstairs, I open my closet and stare at the clothes for a moment, willing something perfect to magically appear. Sundress? Too Pollyanna. Jeans? Too farm. It was obviously wishful thinking when I packed outfits for the club, those would just be over the top here. Tapping my lips thoughtfully with a fingertip, I sift through the options again. *I wish he'd asked me days ago, I could have had something shipped in special, sigh.*

He said casual, and I'm not sure I have a true idea of what 'casual' means. What I *do* know is that I want his eyes to get dark when he sees me, I want him to have to rip them away from my legs. I want to turn him on... *tastefully of course.* I allow myself a small smile.

There will be other men at this street dance, and while I care nothing about their attention, I want Shane to claim me. I want his hands on me, making sure everyone there knows that we are together. *Exactly how 'together' do I want to be? Well that's the question of the evening...I don't know how this grouchy farmer gets so far under my skin.*

It's been a year since my last relationship, and being honest I kept that one at arm's length. By the time I was interested enough to have sex with him, he was over my bullshit. I keep waiting, telling myself that there's one person out there, one perfect person for me. It only takes one, I just didn't think it would be hard to find him. When your life has been handed to you on a silver platter...not finding what you're looking for is...surprising.

I used to indulge in the occasional fling, usually with one of the beautiful men I met on holiday. All of them professed undying love at first sight, I left each with a kiss and a sigh of happiness at their promises. *And every time I walked away I shed a tiny tear for the empty part of me I can't fill.*

Shane is different. Every time his dark eyes catch mine I feel like he can see right into the hidden part of me that is scared I'll never find my someone. His gaze makes me feel vulnerable. I'm not used to it...I don't like it...*I'm afraid he'll see something he doesn't like and walk away.* He's honest, fair, quiet. He doesn't need to throw his weight around, he knows who he is and he doesn't need anyone else to validate him, but you can see respect on the face of every man working for him.

Physically, I crave that man like he's the air I need to breathe. Those tan arms, shoulders corded with muscle. His hands, so strong when he's working, but so gentle when he walks by and gives one of the barn cats a stroke.

Yesterday, I was in the driveway packing up for the day just as he was heading for the house; he pulled off his shirt and used it to wipe the sweat and dirt off his face. The ripple of all those muscles bunching as the sweat trickled towards the waist of his jeans…*those jeans pulled tight over strong thighs, slung low on his hips…swoon.* Every fiber of my being screamed at me to close the distance, run my hands up those abs, bury them in those dark blonde curls and never look back. *But I'm not looking for another fling.*

Cinnamon Kisses

S hane

Pulling up to get Nica, I'm nervous. I want tonight to be fun, I want her to like it here. I don't date much. I kind of quit for a long time when I first brought Katie home, and then I just never took the time. I get out of the truck and walk up the sidewalk. She must have been looking out the window because she opens the door before I can knock.

*Fuck me sideways, those legs...*Nica looks so good I almost forget to breathe. Her dark hair is in a big loose braid pulled over her shoulder, eyes like melted brown sugar staring into mine. Her lips look so soft, she probably has makeup on, but it doesn't look like it. She smells amazing.

It's a warm evening, and her tanned skin glows, she's got kind of a silvery white shirt on, it's got thin lace straps so her shoulders aren't covered, it fits just tight enough and then flares out a little, resting on her hips. She's wearing little navy shorts, they look like they're made of that lace I think is called eyelet. Her legs are long and lean and perfect, all the way down to silver sandals. Her toenails are painted silver too.

She's got a little denim jacket in her hand and as she brings it around her shoulders to put it on, her shirt rides up and I get a glimpse of a perfect tanned stomach. She tucks her phone and a little wallet in the pockets of the coat and smiles at me.

"Hi…you look beautiful." I honestly wish I could stop blurting out whatever is in my fool head when she's around, but she does. She's perfect. She blushes and drops her eyes and then immediately looks back up at me with a small smile.

"Thanks, you look great too," her cool, cultured voice is low and sexy and washes all my nerves away. I turn and we walk to the truck together, I open the door for her and my hand is on the small of her back as she steps up into the truck. Her shirt rides up and my fingers brush bare skin, so smooth. I feel like I'm breathing too loud as I wait for her to tuck her legs in so I can shut the door.

"Hope you don't mind, we're going to make a stop at the school. Katie has theater rehearsal tonight, it's just getting over. I told her I'd give her a ride to the festival," Once we're on the road, I glance at Nica, she looks back at me, smiling.

"Of course, I know she's been working very hard learning her lines." Nica actually does look interested, and I'm glad, Katie idolizes her already.

"Yeah, I can show you around inside quick if you want, she's got some boxes of little prizes to bring, the theater group has a stand in the kid's section of the carnival. She's going to help with that and then meet up with her friends."

We lapse into an easy silence as the truck rumbles down the road. Pulling up to the school, Nica hops out easily and as we walk up the sidewalk she takes my arm. Just natural-like. I wish I'd thought to put an arm around her waist so she'd be closer yet.

Katie is on stage when we quietly walk into the auditorium, she finishes a few lines and then starts talking to the director, who all the kids just call Ms. D. She nods a few times and Ms. D turns to some other students. Katie spots us walking up the aisle and waves.

"Hey Nica! Hey Dad!" She's a bundle of energy, full of smiles. Rehearsal must be going well. Nica's eyes are everywhere, appraising the auditorium and the sets. She smiles widely at Katie.

"Well this is charming, it looks like you guys are working very hard, Katie." Katie smiles at the praise but then her face falls slightly.

"Yeah it looks pretty good, but the school doesn't have much to give Ms. D. for budget, so the sets are really lame. It'll be good though, we're all going to get together tomorrow and hunt through the thrift shop for costumes." Katie laughs as we all walk out to the truck and she hops in the back seat as I give Nica a hand up, "It's probably not as big a production as you had when you were in school," I tense as Katie's vulnerable eyes watch Nica closely.

"Oh, I was never brave enough to do theater," Nica laughs quietly and then turns to look at Katie more seriously.

"What you have to understand though, is that at my boarding school, things were a lot different. Sometimes the big parts went to the talented kids, but a lot of times the big parts went to the highest bidder." Nica smiles to lighten up the mood.

"You're lucky Katie, you got the lead based on talent, and you've got so much you could stand in front of a black curtain in street clothes and you'd still blow that audience away." Nica reaches for the radio dial and finds some music as I glance in the rear-view mirror. Katie is about to burst with pride.

"Will you be able to come to the play, Nica?" her voice is high, nervous.

"I wouldn't miss it, I'll even make sure your dad brings you flowers," Nica gives me a mischievous glance and they laugh. As I laugh along with them, the thought creeps in my head that the play isn't for another month. I've got at least a month with Nica.

We drive up behind all the stalls at the kiddie fair and I help Katie get her boxes to the stand.

"Thanks Dad! Bye! I'm staying at Marissa's tonight, I'll be home tomorrow around lunch, 'kay?" I nod and give her a quick squeeze, dropping a kiss on her blonde curls.

"See ya tomorrow kiddo, be good." She's off with a wave, and I turn and get back in the truck.

"That was real nice of you to say, Katie thinks the world of you," I put the truck in gear and drive around the fairground to the end where they've set up the dance and beer garden, *bet she's never seen one of those either,* parking the truck.

"It's easy to say when every word is true," she murmurs, clicking out of her seatbelt and turning to me. She tilts her head a little and smiles, and I don't know what else she was going to say, but I stop thinking and my hand slides around her waist. Pulling her close I'm kissing those soft lips, she tastes like cinnamon.

I feel her hands slide up my chest and I freeze thinking maybe she's going to push me away. Then I feel one hand making a fist in my shirt, pulling me closer as her other hand slides up into my hair. Her lips part and she's kissing me back. I feel the flick of her tongue on my lower lip and I part my own, sucking hers in lightly, I graze it with my teeth. She leans into me, tugging lightly on my hair, until finally we have to break the kiss to breathe.

Our breath mingles as she rests her forehead lightly to mine, she smiles with her eyes closed. She lets go of my hair and her hand unwinds from my shirt to rest on my chest. She opens her eyes and we smile at each other, I lean in for another kiss, quick and sweet.

"I should have done that a week ago."

Her eyes are liquid, warm and dark, she doesn't close them as she steals a kiss back, then gives me a smile full of promise.

"I wish you would have," she breathes, kissing me once more, long and slow. She reaches over and smooths my shirt, her hand lingering. I cover it with my own, twining my fingers with hers as I kiss her knuckles. What I really want to do right now is start the truck, drive her to the farm, and carry her to my bed. With a small sigh, I let go of her hand, pull the keys and tuck them in my pocket.

"Ready for your first street dance?"

"Yes, and I'd like to see what kind of flowers they grow in the Beer Garden," she grins at me, a sparkle in her eye.

Hopping out of the truck I walk around to her side. Putting my hands on her hips as she steps on the running bar, I lift her down, keeping one arm around her waist.

"I saw this on an old 80's movie once," she says, giving me a sideways glance, and honest-to-god tucks her hand in my back pocket. It's tempting to flex my butt, give her something to play with, but I just laugh and give her a squeeze as we walk through the gates.

A Flower in the Beer Garden

N *ica*

A bored off-duty police officer puts wristbands on us and then Shane's warm hand circles my waist again. He uses the small of my back to guide me through the crowds. I see a lot of smiles, nods and surprised looks as people catch sight of Shane, and from their reaction, I'm happy to be with him. He tucks me in close through the thickest part of the crowd, until we reach a long bar set up at the back of the largest tent.

Shane motions me to one of the few empty bar stools, I try to be sneaky about wiping it off, *it looks weirdly sticky, god I hate vinyl,* sit on it and he stands behind me, warm at my back. He exchanges a few words with the bartender and after a quick joke about the limited options orders us each a beer. Several people stop by, Shane introduces me and we pass several minutes talking.

The people in Gravity are so friendly, and everyone wants a

minute of Shane's time. It's obvious he's well-liked in this tight knit community, and I feel several sets of speculative eyes pass over me as he chats and laughs with everyone. Finishing his conversation, the man he was talking to departs with a wave, chuckling. Shane takes a drink of his own beer, leaning to bump his shoulder lightly against mine.

"Carl's out back helping them roll some more kegs in," he leans close to my ear so I can hear him over the boisterous crowd. "I'm just going to step out there a minute and find out what time he's using the truck tomorrow," Shane gives my shoulder a squeeze. "Band should be starting soon," he rumbles in my ear, "I hope you'll save all your dances for me tonight." His breath tickles across the side of my neck and I give a tiny shiver.

I lean my head back against his shoulder and he tilts his head down thinking I'm going to say something. Instead, I lay a quick kiss on his neck just below his ear, enjoying his reaction as I see his jaw tense and his throat bob as he swallows hard.

"I'll be right here." I smile and he gives me a quick wink and heads around the end of the bar, ducking through an opening in the tent. I continue to sip my beer, letting my eyes wander the tent. Everything I've done here is just so far out of my normal life, it feels so warm and folksy here. Mimsy would absolutely *die* if she knew I was sitting on an old vinyl bar stool in a beer garden right now. *Not that she would know what a beer garden even is in the first place.*

For some reason, everything just feels right. This place is what I need, it grounds me, it's real and dirty and alive. Now that I've been away and can think objectively, my life in the city feels very plastic, shallow, scoured free of what's real and important. I wave at the bartender for another beer, and I can't decide if I'm working myself into a morose funk or having another revelation.

"Well now, what are you doin' here, Bitchy Rich?" My nerves ping right up my spine as Wayne bumps up against me in the process of taking over a newly vacant stool next to me. He studies me for a moment, leering at me, toothpick still in place at the corner of his mouth. *Gross, I hope it's a new one.*

I feel my lip curling as I glance at him, his piggy eyes fixed on me, he flicks his fingers at the bartender then holds up two fingers. The bartender nods and places a shot glass in front of each of us, pours us each a shot of whiskey and leaves the bottle on the bar with a clink. *Well this just got interesting.*

Wayne tosses back his first shot and pours another, watching me for a reaction. I huff out a sigh of annoyance and toss back my first shot as well, he gives a grudging nod of appreciation when I don't choke or cough and refills my glass.

"Did you just stop by to officially welcome me to town?" It's difficult to keep my voice cool, I despise this man.

"Well, I don't know about that, now, I surely don't." Wayne cocks his head, squinting at me. "Stole Wren right out from under my nose, and then, as luck would have it, I got a little visit from the state. They seem to think I'm violatin' some codes... shut the bar down 'til I get things fixed up." He leans closer, hot breath washing over me.

"You wouldn't know anything about that now, would ya honey?" He sucks on the toothpick, then reaches for his second shot, tossing it back.

"Of course I do, you lecherous ingrate," Wayne's eyes widen, he wasn't expecting me to admit I had a part in shutting down his shitty bar. I give him a cold smirk and down my second shot, enjoying the burn. I bite back a gasp when a heavy forearm bumps me from behind. Glancing over my shoulder, a huge man has just pushed up to the bar behind me, he grins at Wayne over my head. *You have got to be fucking kidding me, Wayne brought in some sort of muscle, this is priceless. Well...in for a penny, in for a pound I guess.*

Spinning my stool away from Wayne, I face the newcomer. He's tall, as tall as Shane I'd guess, and his shoulders are almost as wide. His dark brown hair is cropped tight to his head, and his eyes are actually kind of a startling shade of blue. He doesn't look friendly as he stares down at me, his square jaw is tight, muscles tensing, he's completely nailing his 'intimidation' look.

"Hi, we haven't met, I'm Nica," I keep my voice bright, sticking out my hand between us. He's thrown off, and he takes my hand, giving it a careful shake.

"Hank" he grunts and then his brain catches up and he drops my hand like a hot coal, but the damage is done. He's not scary. I give Hank an exaggerated look over, mentally taking his measurements as he stares at me fiercely. When I don't react, he glances over my head at Wayne, mutely looking for instruction.

"Well Hank, I'll tell you this, with that jawline and those baby blue eyes, I think you've missed your calling." His eyes are back to mine like I flipped a switch, and I drag a finger quickly down his arm. He twitches, startled and I hear Wayne sigh behind me. I lean up to Hank, speaking in a sultry whisper.

"That jaw and the abs I'm guessing you're hiding under that shirt should be on the cover of a steamy romance, Hank, you could be famous." At this point I may as well have just smacked Hank in the forehead with a hammer, he's standing there dumbfounded, cheeks flaming. With a smile, I spin my stool back to face Wayne. He waves Hank off with a flick of his thick fingers, exasperated.

"Good call Wayne, that was fun." I take a sip of my beer, waiting.

"He's my idiot nephew and I shoulda known better," Wayne mutters, "But that don't change nothin'." His eyes are angry as he stares at me.

"I don't like rich bitches that don't know their place," Wayne leans towards me, the toothpick in his mouth bobbing with every word. "The way I see it, you cost me a ton of mo-" he cuts off with a strangled little wheeze glancing over my head. At the same time I feel warmth at my back and hear Shane's deep voice.

"Evening Wayne, thanks for keeping Nica company," his voice is friendly, and he loops one arm across my chest, leaning me back into him in a clearly possessive move. With his other hand he taps my beer. I glance up at him with a smile, letting him take the lead. I like where this is going.

"Mind if I share?" He gives me a little wink that pings me right in the lady bits. I silently offer him the beer, enjoying the weight of his arm, his heat at my back, and Wayne's discomfort. Obviously Wayne is like all bullies, not going to keep picking at me when a bigger dog arrives on the scene. *It's a shame actually, I was just starting to have some fun with poor Wayne. He thinks he's a big fish, he just doesn't realize he's in a fishbowl.*

"Evening Shane," Wayne tries for a smile but ends up looking mostly constipated, "it was no chore at all, you know me, can't resist talking to a pretty girl." Standing up off the bar stool, he digs in his pocket and tosses some money on the bar.

"Myrna bringing her chocolate cake Sunday?" Shane takes a drink of my beer then offers it back to me.

"I expect she'll bring it," Wayne barks out a laugh, "wouldn't be Sunday dinner without that damn cake."

"That is a fact," Shane chuckles.

"You two lovebirds have a good evening," Wayne taps the bar twice with the flat of his hand and then sketches a wave as he ambles away. I take a drink of beer and offer it back to Shane.

"Sunday dinner?" The confusion in my voice is obvious.

"Sunday dinner at Aunt Sheila's, I was going to see if you wanted to come with me." Shane's eyes are dancing with amusement, "We eat a big meal, drink some beer and play yard games, it's a good time, and the weather looks fine."

"And Wayne will be there because…"

"Well, because Sheila would be pissed if he didn't show," Shane is clearly trying not to laugh at this point. "She is his mother after all." *Oh fuck a duck they're cousins.*

"Isn't the saying, 'You can't choose your family'?" Shane chuckles. "He'll be alright now, he needed a kick in the pants about that bar anyway, and you were obviously the right person for that job." His tone turns serious and he gives me a squeeze and then letting me go, running a hand through his hair as I turn to look up at him.

"Don't worry, if I hear he hires any more girls too young to be around all that, I'll just make sure Myrna hears about it, she'll kick his ass so hard it'll look like he grew another head." I blurt out a laugh at that mental picture and he laughs along with me.

Shane slides a hand around my waist, under the hem of my shirt, hot on the sensitive skin of my stomach. His thumb swirls a light pattern on my ribs. His skin is so perfectly rough, and the intimacy of his touch is heightened by the noise and the crowd. No one can see his hand, gently making every nerve in my body line up like iron filings to a magnet.

I love the way he can't seem to stop touching me, I can't

get over the heat of him, the feel of his hands on my skin. It surprises me, honestly. I feel like staying in Gravity is changing me, making my life a more visceral experience.

The heat of Georgia, *the humidity,* the dirt of the farm, the animals, the people, *so very different from the traffic and noise of the city*, it's almost overwhelming sometimes. It's just so much *life,* and yet, it is so peaceful. The way people work, play and live here; it makes me feel like I've missed something, living in a little bubble of concrete and champagne.

Before I met Shane I was not even *close* to being a 'touchy-feely' person. I have long preferred to keep people at a distance. Shane is like an addiction. Every touch, every brush of his fingers, his lips, his body close enough to feel the heat rolling off him in waves…I want it all…I want more.

Wren wanders up at that moment, hanging on the arm of a short guy with spiky white blonde hair that must be Mike. He looks like he was probably a jock in high school, muscular, cute, showing off for Wren like a strutting peacock. Behind them is another man who looks a couple of years older, maybe mid-20s. He's got red hair with gold streaks winding through it as if he spends a lot of time outdoors, a full beard and he is *big.* Shane is a big guy, but the redhead is a *giant.*

"Having a good night boss?" Mike's natural voice is probably not as low as he's trying to make it. Shane turns to look at them and smiles easily.

"Evening Mike, Wren, Kane," he nods at each of them, "It's a beautiful evening and I hear the band playing, I think we're going to head out for a dance."

Shane's easy drawl makes me want to melt. I feel nice and warm in my belly, and the drinks I've had are letting that easy-dizzy-fuzzy feeling take hold of my brain.

"Let's dance," I agree, taking his hand and leading him towards the music.

Darlin' Let's Dance

S hane

Nica winds her fingers through mine and my eyes follow the sway of her hips and the flutter of that shimmery shirt as she leads. We reach a spot somewhere in the middle of the crowd and she spins around to face me. The beat of the music is fast, pounding through the speakers, but she steps close, and her arms slide around my waist.

Smiling, I wrap my arms around her, sliding one hand down to hover on the top curve of her ass. After a minute or so, the music slows down as the singer starts rasping out a love song. I feel her fingers playing along the muscles of my back as she rests her cheek on my chest. Bending my head down, I let my lips touch her hair. It smells like peaches. Her perfume is something deep and sexy and I just breathe her in as we sway to the music. *I don't ever want to stop holding this woman.*

Lightly running my hand up and down her back, I hear a

hum of pleasure from Nica as I find the hem of her shirt and my fingers touch her skin. The music changes again but she doesn't pull away, we just keep dancing, nice and slow. Nica fits against my body like the piece I didn't know was missing.

We dance until the band takes a break and I keep an arm around her waist as we head to one of the picnic tables lining the sides of the street. Sitting down, I straddle the bench and she sits in front of me, her side up close to my chest. Loose strands of her hair tickle my neck as a light breeze kicks up.

"Hey y'all," Wren's high sweet voice pipes up behind us and she comes around the table, Mike following close behind, "mind if we sit?" I smile at them both as they find seats across the table. Kane shows up silently a minute later, he's huge, but he moves like a shadow. He looks at the space left at the table for a second and quirks an eyebrow at Wren when she scoots a little to make room.

"I'm gonna grab another beer, anyone need one?" He rumbles, looking around, Mike nods yes to another beer, and Kane heads to the bar. Nica smiles at Wren.

"Having a good time, Wren?" Nica shifts to turn a little towards Wren, her butt scooting back on the bench to press firmly against my dick. *Well there goes standing up anytime soon, thank fuck it's pretty dark.* I let my fingers trail along her thigh, playing with the edge of her shorts near her ass where Wren won't see. I hide a smile as I feel goosebumps dotting her skin.

They start chatting easily, not expecting me to chime in, and my attention wanders back to the kiss in my truck. I wonder how she sees tonight ending.

A Not-at-all-Glamorous Detour

N^{ica}

Wren and I talk for a while as Shane's fingers slide in a lazy pattern on the back of my thigh. Eventually, Mike grabs Wren's hand and twirls her back out to the dance floor.

Two local women who look well into their 40's giggle like teenagers as they approach Kane. He good-naturedly allows one of them to tug him out to the dance floor without saying a word. I feel Shane shift behind me, leaning forward he rests his chin on my shoulder.

"Ready to get out of here?" His voice is a whisper full of heat, and my throat tightens up so fast my 'yes' is the barest whisper. Shifting on the bench, I scoot away from him just a little, and as I start to stand up, I feel a searing pain in the tender flesh just below the crease of my ass, high up on my leg.

Biting back a gasp, I surreptitiously feel the back of my leg as I turn towards him smiling. There's nothing there, and I'm not bleeding. *Probably some fucking bug, it probably laid eggs, oh my god.* It still hurts but it'll have to just wait until I get somewhere with a mirror, I'm not going to ruin this moment. Letting him pull me close, I wrap an arm around his waist and we head for his truck.

Sitting on the seat of the truck turns what was a dull sting back into a white hot pain, and I can't stop a little whimper. Shane looks at me carefully as we drive through town.

"You okay? Something wrong?" His hand slides over my knee comfortingly, but this thing in the back of my leg fucking hurts. *Oh my god what if it's a stinger?*

"Um, yeah, everything's fine," we hit a bump in the road that makes me bounce on the seat and I let out another humiliating little whimper, "...except back at the dance I'm pretty sure some kind of bug stung me...can you take me to my place? I need to see if there's a stinger in there or something." I'm dying a little with every word, I feel like such an idiot. I've got some kind of egg laying stinger in my ass, I'm just sure of it as it stings and throbs. *This is not a glamorous way to die.*

Reality Check

*S*hane

A stinger? I have no idea what could have bitten her, maybe there was a wasp under the bench or something. Something happened anyway, she's shifting uncomfortably and her smile is forced. It only takes a couple of minutes to get to her place. Unlocking the door, she tosses her jacket on a nearby chair, kicks her sandals off quickly, and heads up the stairs, presumably to her bathroom.

"Grab a drink if you like, I'll just be a minute," she waves a hand at the kitchen before she disappears. I wander out to the kitchen and take a look in the fridge. There's a couple bottles of white wine, one open, some cheese that looks smelly and expensive, and part of a loaf of bread. One whole shelf is full of bottles of water, so I go that route. Cracking one open I shut the fridge and go look out the window to her back yard.

"Um, Shane?" I hear Nica's voice filtering down the stairs

a few minutes later, and I walk quickly back out to the main room. Looking up the stairs, I don't see her, but I hear her voice again.

"So, this is quite possibly the most awkward thing I've ever had to do on a date…but could you come up and look at this?" Her voice is trembling, and as I climb the stairs and see her standing just inside the bathroom by a clean white counter, her face is flaming with embarrassment.

"Okay, let me see it, where does it hurt?" I am so fucking proud of how steady my voice is at this point, because Nica has taken off her shorts and is standing there in a tiny cotton robe that falls just a few inches below her ass.

Nica raises the edge of the robe on the left side revealing half of a perfect ass cheek. I see the black lace edge of her underwear, a sexy line angling up to her hip, and feel a little rush of heat in my chest. She leans forward a little, her other hand on the counter, and our eyes meet in the mirror.

Dropping carefully to my knees behind her I lean down and smooth a hand over the back of her thigh, and immediately see the problem.

"Do you see anything? Is it a stinger? Or a bug? Oh my god, does anything around here lay eggs with a stinger?" Her voice is bordering on hysterical and I can't help but laugh a little, *egg laying stinger,* as I look back up at her frantic face in the mirror.

"Darlin', you can relax. What you've got here is a splinter in your ass." Nica stares at me as if I stopped speaking English. "Do you have a tweezer or something? I'll get it out for you." I grin at her in the mirror and her face flames with embarrassment.

"Do I have tweezers?" Snorting delicately, she pulls open one of the cabinets behind us where four tweezers of varying angles and sharpness are lined up with all of her other girl-tools. Giggling softly she waves a hand at the selection. "These are all virgins in the splinter-pulling department, use whichever ones you think will be best."

"Fair enough," I laugh, looking at the options carefully for a second before selecting one. She turns around and puts her hands on the counter bending forward slightly. *Lord have mercy.* I drop to my knees behind her again and skim my hands up the backs of her thighs. *I just don't want her to jump when I touch her with sharp tweezers, that's all...not because her skin is smooth and soft and I just want to touch her...*

I lean in close enough that she must feel my breath, because her skin bursts into goosebumps. I gently push on her skin close to the splinter and blow out a little breath.

"Okay, here we go, it'll probably come right out so just hold real still, darlin'." I lean around her hip finding her eyes in the mirror. She mutely bobs her head yes and then squeezes her eyes shut, ready for it to hurt. I hear her bite back a little gasp when I pull the splinter out, followed by a laugh of instant relief when it's gone.

"Is it all out? Can I see it?" I laugh and hold up the tweezer, dropping the splinter in her outstretched palm. It's about half an inch long, maybe the size of a pencil lead.

"How disappointing...it stung bad enough I was expecting something at least the size of my finger," she gripes and I laugh louder. Looking over my shoulder in the cabinet I find some astringent and grab a cotton ball out of the container on the counter. She lets out a hiss and then falls silent as I clean the spot, and then I can't help myself, I lean forward and press my lips to the curve of her ass.

"A kiss to make it better?" I find her eyes again in the mirror, smiling as I stand up. *I want her. I want to kiss every inch of her skin and then make her mine.*

"Mmhmm, I like that," she murmurs, lips quirked up in a sexy grin, "I guess you can add that to my list of firsts, splinter in the ass, check." Looking again at the little splinter in her palm, she leans over and drops it in the trash.

"This town has been full of firsts for me," Nica muses, "first splinter, could have skipped that, first picnic table, street dance, beer garden, farm, dirt road, cotton field..." she continues, ticking things off on her fingers, distracted. Not realizing every word is a knife in my heart. *She doesn't belong here. Fuck. I'm just a way to pass time until she can get back to the city and laugh about this with her friends.*

"...homemade peach pie," giving a little hum of pleasure, she reaches out and laces her fingers in mine. Turning she begins to lead me down a short hall. Once I'm through the doorway of the bathroom, I stop, her fingers leaving mine with a little jerk. *I can't do this, I can't just be a distraction and then let her go.* She turns back to me, surprised.

"This isn't a good idea," I force the words out, throat tight, "this won't work, I'm sorry." I don't look at her again as I walk rigidly down the stairs, ignoring the hurt and confusion in her voice as she calls my name once. I don't stop to put my boots on, just grab them and walk out to my truck. Smacking the steering wheel hard with my palm I start the truck and roar away from the curb without glancing back.

My heart feels like a rock in my chest. I'm an idiot for thinking that maybe she was starting to like being here...with me. I thought she was enjoying being away from the stress of the city and her life there, but she probably misses it like crazy. To her this is just a backward little town and she's stuck here. It's stupid… we went on one fucking date, and here I was, starting to think about keeping her forever.

Roaring up the lane, I park the truck, throw my boots on the porch and stomp into the house. I'm glad Katie's staying with a friend, I wouldn't be good company tonight.

So...

Nica

What the ever-loving-fuck just happened...

Back to Business

N^{ica}

For the next three days I avoid the farm. I spent the rest of that miserable night trying to figure out where we went wrong, and how I can fix it, but I can't make myself call him. What if he just didn't want me? Maybe he was just thinking I would be a fling, here and then gone, and it's not worth the trouble. Whatever his hang-up, maybe he did me a favor. I'm not in the mood for a fling, I want something real. *Something forever.*

I throw myself into my work. My mother is pleased at the progress of the Organics line, and she's started throwing me more involved marketing strategies to get underway. She greets my idea of opening an office with more enthusiasm than I expected.

"Darling, what a marvelous idea! A headquarters in the heart of the country," Evelyn is practically gushing, it makes me nervous. "Make sure you choose something with some history, something marketable. You have carte blanche! Talk soon!" She rings off before I can utter another word. *I'm fine Mother, thanks for asking.*

Calling Tara, I have her locate someone with good knowledge of historical buildings to walk through the one I saw up for auction soon. I jog by the building almost every day, I want it.

That handled for now, I turn to the other project I've had on a back burner for a day or so. It doesn't matter that Shane doesn't want me, *that's a lie, it hurts so fucking bad I can't breathe, but I can't deal with that right now.*

Katie is the lead in the school play, and the sets are crap due to serious lack of funding. The funding part is easy to solve with a phone call to my lawyer. Thirty minutes and a very happy superintendent of schools later, I am an anonymous donor supporting the theater program, including a scholarship fund. It feels good to put some of my money into something important to Katie.

Tara texts to let me know I'm going to meet a man named Charles, an expert in historical renovation, later this afternoon. I spend the next few hours working on plans and scheduling a crew for the week and then head downtown.

Charles is a burly man in his 50s, thick black hair shot through with silver and an easy manner that seems to be the norm in Georgia.

"Call me Chuck, nice to meet you Nica," his hand is rough and warm as he squeezes mine briefly. We spend some time looking at the outside of the building, and then the estate agent arrives and lets us inside. It's a hastily cleaned up mess, the floor has been cleared of trash but is still covered with a heavy layer of dust and smaller debris.

I'm happy to see the stained glass windows surrounding the double door entrance have remained intact, and I can see that with refinishing the wood floors will be lovely. Chuck does some poking at the ceiling and beams at me when he knocks one of the awful 80's drop ceiling tiles out of the way to expose a beautiful tin ceiling several feet above.

The second story is rougher, heavy beams and wood floors, it's all wide open and will clean up beautifully. The exposed brick walls and tall windows at the front of the building lend character and good light, I can't wait to see the windows clean and the floors shining. We mount rickety stairs to the third story and Chuck and I just stand there silently for a moment.

"This must have been living quarters for someone with money a long time ago," Chuck can hardly contain his excitement, "just look at that double-sided marble fireplace and those skylights! The bookshelves even look original!" He walks around the space, muttering excitedly. The fireplace is in the center of the main room. One section of the huge space has built in bookshelves covering the side walls. There are three large skylights built into the roof at intervals, each has six panes of glass and a crank and pulley system to open them.

The back of the third floor is a bathroom with a huge clawfoot tub that sets Chuck off on another round of excited muttering and note-taking. A pedestal sink and a toilet that has a tank up close to the ceiling with a chain to flush are also intact. There's another of the amazing skylights above the tub.

Chuck beams when I tell him that I really want to embrace the history of the place. The downtown area has a number of the original buildings still in use and intact, it's actually a strong historical district for a town this size. I want to contribute to that, help it grow. *Why...why do I care...I'll get this up and running and Mother will probably send me somewhere else anyway...if I let her...*

If I let her...*ohmygod,* the minute the thought crosses my mind, I excuse myself and let Chuck keep looking around. Leaning against the brick wall on the second floor, I force myself to think about leaving. Do I want to go back to the city? *No.* As the truth reverberates through my brain, I almost feel sick to my stomach.

I've fallen in love with this place...*and a man who doesn't love me back.* Fuck that noise. This is the life I didn't know I was looking for, it's time to make it happen.

Retail Therapy

*S*hane

I better get out of this funk or I'm going to have guys quitting on me. I know I've been an asshole for the past few days, and I can't seem to stop the biting comments and derisive grunts that shoot out of my mouth. Even Carl, as easy going as they come, has started to avoid me. So far I'm trying to shove away my feelings by working late until I fall into bed, too tired to dream.

It's not working. Everyday I second guess walking out of Nica's house. Every hour, I analyze all the things she said and what she really meant. All this thinking gets me nowhere. I'm not getting into a relationship with someone who's only here for a little while. I owe it to Katie not to do that, and she likes Nica already, I'm not going to hurt their friendship by adding in a messy relationship that has to end.

To make matters worse, Katie has a major event, *in the very scary girly category,* coming up and she's freaking out, which freaks me out. It's three weeks until her Junior Prom and she hasn't got a dress yet. She's tried on every single one of the limited options in town. She's made me come along and give my opinion which was more comical than anything.

I don't really understand the problem. She's a 17 year old girl, she's slim, she has pretty blonde hair, it seems like she could throw on damn near anything and look nice. She actually growled at me when I said those very words though, and then she cried. I told her my wallet is open and backed away from the whole thing.

She's been hanging out with this boy, Miles, quite a bit, and he's her prom date. I don't know if they've hit boyfriend/girlfriend status, but she seems to like him. He's polite and always a little nervous around me, so I like him well enough. He called her last night to ask what color her dress was so he could order a corsage, and that brought on a whole flurry of panic all over again.

I'm pretty sure she told him just to get her white or silver so they'd go with whatever she gets, but it's time to go shopping again. I told her as soon as she gets out of school today I'll pick her up and she can comb through all the options in town one more time. If that doesn't work, we'll drive to the big mall about two hours down the road next week. I asked her if we could order one of everything she likes online, but she freaked out again, I have no idea why.

I text Carl to meet me at the home farm, and he rumbles up in his ancient truck a few minutes later. I made a stop at the meat locker in town and grabbed a bunch of steaks. Another stop to the grocery store for beer. Carl walks up to me like I'm a bear with a sore paw and I grimace, *yeah, I've been an asshole.*

"I've got some stuff to do, have to take Katie shopping for a prom dress," we both laugh, he knows how bad I don't want to do this. "Call the guys, tell them to knock off early tonight and give everybody a pack of steaks and a six-pack to take home." Carl nods and I get a real smile out of him for the first time in days.

"You got it, Boss," we don't need to say much else. We've been friends a long time.

An hour later I'm sitting in my truck at the curb as Katie comes bouncing out of the school. I'm cussing myself out because if I'd got busy and got her a new car, instead of waiting on insurance when she hit a deer a couple months ago, she'd be driving herself and I wouldn't be going shopping right now.

Her friend Olive is with her, I like Olive, she seems real nice, she's quiet and thoughtful, probably a good choice for dress opinions. I'm just glad she doesn't have Samantha in tow, *that* girl could talk the paint off a barn.

"You coming along to help get this girl a dress?" I joke with Olive as they climb in the truck.

"Yes, sir," Olive lets out a little giggle, "She's been driving us all crazy, she's so picky!" Katie lets out an affronted huff quickly followed by a giggle of her own.

"Oh stuff it, both of you," Katie laughs, "today is the day. I can *feel* it."

"Well then, let us get this show on the road," I pull away from the curb and Katie starts fiddling with the dials for some music. Windows down, sun's shining, I think she's right.

Fairy Godmother Vibes

N ica

Chuck and I have been through every nook and cranny of the building, *well, he has, I peeked in every nook and cranny and decided they were probably full of spiders.* I put him in touch with my lawyer so that they can figure out all the details. Chuck will attend the auction for me, the building will be mine soon.

Work will begin immediately, and a significant part of the renovation will be the third story living quarters. I'm moving in as soon as it's ready. I'm in love with everything about this building and the idea of a downtown loft in a town the size of Gravity has a sort of delicious irony.

Charles heads for his truck with a wave. The estate agent heads for her car as well, excited at the prospect of a serious buyer coming to the auction. She'll keep a lid on it as much as she can, but I don't doubt I'll get to pay top dollar for the property. It's worth it to me, and this one will be a business expense, *I amuse myself sometimes.*

"Nica? Hey! What're you doing here?" Katie and a friend are ambling up the sidewalk arm in arm.

"Well hello Katie, I was just wrapping up some business, what are you girls doing on this beautiful day?" I scan the area behind them but Shane isn't here. Good. *I wish he was. Shut up, heart.*

"I'm shopping for a prom dress, it's been awful, there's nothing cool or new in the stores here, and I don't want to order anything online, because Maisie Johnson did, and the seams busted at Homecoming because it was cheap, and it dyed her skin blue all over her stomach, and she got a rash." Katie's words tumble out in a rush, her friend nodding beside her. "This is Olive by the way, Olive, this is Nica, she's working with my dad on a big project at the farm."

Olive is a slim girl with shoulder length brown hair, glasses and a friendly smile. She checks me out surreptitiously, waiting for Katie to take the lead.

"Anyway, I guess we're going to go look through one more time, if we don't find something, Dad says we'll head to the mall in the city next week, he's across at the hardware store now." She waves a hand across the street and my heart does a quick little flip. I turn to look and there he is, just leaving the store. I give myself a quick pep-talk, I thought I'd have more time to prepare before I saw him again.

Shane slows just a bit when he sees me, and then walks up with a smile that doesn't quite reach his eyes. *Ouch.*

"Afternoon Nica, Katie telling you about her dress problems?" His voice is friendly, but that's it, I could be a guy from the hardware store and he would sound the same. *Fine, we'll get there the hard way I guess.*

"She is, and if it's alright with you, I'd love to help." I keep my voice bright, friendly, *downright chipper*. Katie gives a little squeal of happiness.

"Oh that would be so awesome, maybe you can find something I didn't see!" She's bouncing on her toes with excitement. *At Betty's Bargain Barn? SoFabBoutik? Highly unlikely.*

"Actually, Katie, the best way I could help is by bringing the shopping to you," Katie looks at me, confused, and I continue. "Honestly you'd be doing me a favor, I love shopping. I tell you what, I'll have some things shipped here, and I'll bring them to the farm for you to take a look at, sound fun?"

Katie lets out a little shriek and dives at me for a hug.

"OMG that would be amazing, like, *amazing*, I can't even, eeeee!" Katie and Olive begin talking excitedly. I pull out my phone and quickly take a couple photos of Katie. Shane pulls out his wallet, handing Katie some money.

"Well, if I'm out of shopping, you girls may as well go grab an ice cream, I'll meet you back at the truck."

"Sweet! Thanks Dad! After that can you drop us at Olive's? I'm staying over tonight, remember? We've got that Spanish trip and we have to leave at the butt crack of dawn," she grimaces comically, "See ya Nica, How long do you think it will take?? Oh it doesn't matter, sorry that's rude, I'll be back Sunday morning! See ya!" Katie grabs the money and links her arm with Olive again as they head up the street.

And just like that we're alone together. We both laugh, watching Katie and Olive leave in a flurry of chatter, and then Shane is quiet, staring at me. and I lift my chin defiantly.

"What are you doing, Nica?" He doesn't sound mad, just... resigned?

"I'm giving Katie every girl's dream for prom, Shane. She will go to that dance in a custom dress and she will feel amazing." I seal my lips shut before I say anything else. *Like totally unrelated to prom things, about us, and how much I want there to be an 'us', and how he needs to get over whatever is holding him back and get on board.*

"Well…thank you. I guess I'm clearly out of my element with prom stuff," he scruffs a hand over his stubbly jaw and glances at me again, giving me that grin that always sends a white hot flash straight south. *Down girl, he just smiled for fuckssake.*

"You're welcome." I don't know what else to say.

"Okay then, I guess I better go meet the girls. It was good to see you Nica." His eyes hold mine for a moment and then he turns and walks away. It hurts my heart, and I want to grab him and kiss him…and slap him for shutting things down before we even got started, and then kiss him.

An Evening Jog

N^{ica}

"V! Babe! I've missed you *so* much!" It's hard not to roll my eyes at that, but I'm calling in a favor so it's time to be gracious. I intentionally called late morning so she'd be up...but only two or three mimosas deep.

"Mims, I need you to take care of something for me," I pause, waiting to hear what kind of mood she's in.

"Anything darling! You know me! Always got your back girl!" The magnanimous lovey mood...perfect. I quickly outline the situation with Katie, leaving out that Katie's dad has me all hot and bothered. Mimsy's second husband is a formal wear designer of some note. He's dressed a number of celebrities for red carpet, so I know he'll have some options for me. I text Mimsy the pictures of Katie so she can gauge size and best silhouette.

"Oh, darling, she is *lovely*," Mimsy gushes, "this is going to be fun! It's like having my own daughter for an afternoon!" *She might be more than three deep.* "Do you want me to send jewelry? Hair pieces? Shoes?"

"Send it all Mims. Just don't forget she's 17 and a very sweet girl with a very protective father, keep the neckline and the leg slit safe." This is going to be amazing.

"Yes, yes, sweet and safe, oh *look* at her big blue eyes! I'm on it. Ciao darling." She disconnects and I toss my phone aside with a sigh. Helping Katie is easy, Shane, on the other hand, is an itch I can't scratch. Flopping back on the couch, I stare at the ceiling, looking for answers. I doze off and dream of Shane walking away.

When I jerk awake, the shadows in the room have all moved and I'm disoriented. Glancing at my phone, I've been out for almost four hours. I laugh quietly to myself, it was definitely a stress nap. Shaking out the cobwebs, I throw on workout clothes and go for a run.

Lost in my own thoughts as my shoes pound a steady rhythm on the pavement, I look around and realize my path is leading to the farm. I hesitate for a beat and then, feeling a burst of determination, I keep running. The last part is a gravel road. Crossing the bridge, the big old farmhouse coming into view over the rise by the river. It's almost sunset, I should turn around and head back. I don't.

Jogging up the lane, it's quiet, the usual array of trucks and cars are gone. It's a Saturday night, everyone must be done for the day. Stopping at the pump, I get a drink, *add drinking out of a water spigot to the list of firsts...*

I've come this far and I'm not turning back now, I need to talk to Shane. Barney's tail gives a half-hearted thump as I walk by the front porch. I give his head a pat and stroke his long soft ears a minute, finding my courage. I'm going to knock on that door, I'm going to get Shane to come out and talk to me, and I'm not leaving until he tells me why he left. Yes I am, that is what I am going to do. Right now. Now. *Traitorous feet aren't listening.*

Petting the dog for another second, I finally square my shoulders and head around the house to the side porch. My eyes are on the sidewalk, not wanting to trip over one of the ten or so barn cats that tend to mosey over to the house in the evenings.

As I step onto the porch, the sound of running water registers in my brain for the first time and I freeze. Slowly turning my gaze to the outdoor shower, my heart starts pounding wildly. *Shane.*

His back is to me, hands braced on the far wall of the shower as he lets the water pound those amazing shoulders and the back of his neck. The walls of the shower start at his muscular calves and cover to the middle of his broad chest. There's a curtain that can be pulled for more privacy, but he hasn't bothered. Ohhhh...*Katie is on her Spanish trip...he's alone.*

Because Why?

S hane

Hearing a noise behind me, I pull my head out of the stream of the shower, wiping the water out of my eyes and shoving my hair back as I turn. Nica stands there, looking at me. Her cheeks redden as I jump, startled.

"Nica? What's wrong, did something happen? I didn't hear your car." I'm looking around as if the emergency that brought her here will present itself, and my brain registers the workout clothes she's wearing and the light sheen of sweat on her forehead and chest.

"No, nothing, everything's fine, I was just out running...and I wanted to talk to you." Her voice is firm and quiet, her eyes fix on my chest and in the dim light they seem to darken.

"Um, sure..." I look at the towel I left hanging on a chair several feet away, *that was poor planning.* She doesn't seem to notice, she's chewing absently on her lower lip, upset.

"Why did you walk out?" The words tumble out of her mouth as if she's afraid to say them. A hard knot forms in my chest, she's hurting too, and it's my fault. Suddenly, I'm angry, not at her, but at the situation, and I can't stop the words from pouring out.

"I left because your list of first things might be a cute joke, but I can't start something with you just so you can go back to the city and tell your friends about checking 'fuck a country boy' off your bucket list." Shoving my wet hair back again, I keep talking even though her mouth has dropped open in outrage and my brain is screaming at me to shut up.

"You come here and you're beautiful, and you're smart, and everyone thinks you're amazing, but what they forget is that someday you'll leave." My chest is heaving with emotion and I realize I'm yelling. "You'll leave and go back to your city life, and this will all be an amusing story you tell your friends over cocktails!"

Whatever. It's out there, and she's not saying anything, so I'm right.

"You fucking idiot, Shane, you don't know anything," my eyes widen at the words hissing furiously out of her mouth. Nica turns on her heel and storms into the dark.

"You'll leave and take a piece of me with you and I'll be broken," my heart whispers after her.

The Shower

ica

Angry tears blur my vision as I run down the lane. I pause at the end, realizing I've just dedicated myself to a jog home, partly on a gravel road, in the dark.

I hear a motor and see a headlight bouncing over the lane behind me, and hastily pat my eyes dry before crossing my arms over my chest and assuming the bitchiest look I can muster. *I am not crying over Shane and I am not some fucking damsel in distress.* I'm also not going to do something idiotic like run away. I don't run away from anything. *Except naked men in showers saying all the wrong things, they make me run away...apparently.*

Shane is moving fast, but as soon as he spots me slows way down and approaches at a crawl on one of the four-wheelers. His hair is still dripping, he's got jeans and boots on, but no shirt. Under any other circumstances I would appreciate this very much, every inch of him is lickable perfection, but I'm pissed. I suck in a breath and open my mouth, ready to unload all my frustration and hurt feelings but he speaks first.

"Don't leave me, not like this…" his voice is low and tense and his eyes find mine as he sucks in a breath, "…not ever." I feel my anger fading fast and my heart is pounding in my chest. I open my mouth as my brain tries to form a coherent thought. The little 'huh?' I utter is humiliating.

"I didn't mean any of that, I mean, I know I said it, but it's what I'm most afraid of, and I threw it on you, and I shouldn't have," he sighs, frustrated. "I never should have walked out your door that night. I should have taken every minute I could get and been thankful for them when you left me someday." He's staring at me like I'm the air he needs to breathe. "I should have asked you to stay with me." *My heart just melted, my underpants are on fire, I'm sweaty and dusty, and that man just said every word I ever needed to hear.*

He's off the four-wheeler and closes the gap between us before I can find words. His hands slide into my hair, bunching it up in his fists as he yanks my head back just hard enough to pull a sigh of pleasure from my lips. His kiss is almost hard enough to bruise, and I can't get enough. I part my lips, letting his tongue swipe past mine, sucking in his bottom lip and biting it gently. He groans and one of his hands lets loose of my hair and skims down my back to my ass. Breaking the kiss to breathe, he hugs me in close, burying his face in my neck.

"Stay with me tonight," he murmurs, squeezing me again before straightening, looking into my eyes. "Please." Putting my fears in a box and locking it up tight, I nod at him solemnly. We have tomorrow to talk about the future, I have tomorrow to tell him I'm here to stay. Tonight we will live in this moment without the burden of planning or thinking too hard.

Lacing his fingers through mine, he leads me to the four-wheeler and I climb on behind him, wrapping my arms around his waist. I rest my cheek on his broad back and close my eyes, happy in this uncomplicated moment.

The ride back to the house is much faster than the angry walk that led me away, Shane pulls the four-wheeler up near the porch, turning on the seat to kiss me before we get off. He kicks his boots off and looks at me, hands on the button of his jeans, his eyes are so dark.

"There should be plenty of hot water left." Shane cocks an eyebrow questioningly. *Ohhhh yeah.* I smile and he turns on the water and shucks his jeans. He stands still a moment and glances at me as I take him in, *now is NOT the time to hyperventilate, but daaaamn*, then he steps closer and reaches out to help me undress.

He slides the armband that holds my phone down my arm and carefully sets it on the shelf. His fingers pull the hem of my tank up over my head gracefully enough and then I utter a nervous giggle at the idea of him helping me with a sports bra. My laugh surprises him, bringing his eyes back to my face, and then he looks at the sports bra again, his hands hovering in mid-air.

"Yeah, I'm gonna let you handle that," he chuckles, the tension is broken. I giggle again and shimmie out of my sports bra and leggings as gracefully as I'm able, as he kindly turns towards the house and flips off the outdoor light. Tossing my clothes on a nearby chair, I turn back to Shane and stare for a moment. The moonlight is shining through the clouds and our skin looks blue in the darkness, lit only by the moon. Every plane of his muscular chest looks chiselled from stone in this light, I'm aching to run my hands over him.

The evening air is mild, but when a light breeze stirs, I shiver. Shane holds out a hand and pulls me into the shower. There's a large waterfall head above us, and we face each other. He pushes the wet hair back from my face and I wrap my arms around his waist and explore the muscles of his back. He leans down for a lingering kiss before nudging me to turn around. His hands are in my hair, shampooing it carefully, and as I lean back and let the water rinse the suds away, his hands slide around my ribcage to cup my breasts. His hips press up behind me, and I feel the heat of him, pinned hard against my ass. His hands squeeze and slip over my nipples as I lean my head back against his shoulder with a little moan of pleasure.

One of his hands leaves and then returns holding a bar of soap that smells amazing. *Note to self, find out where that soap came from, okay, now shut up brain.* I shut my eyes, raising my face to the spray, and give myself over to the sensation of Shane washing my body.

I have never felt anything as deeply sensual as his hands and the soap, slowly washing every bit of me. When he reaches my butt, he moves the soap in slow circles on each cheek, almost tickling the sensitive skin. Moving to my back, the water washes the suds down, naturally funneling them to the crack of my ass, and I feel his cock start sliding up and down in a gentle rhythm.

He reaches around and begins slow circles on my belly, one breast, then the other, his fingers gentle as they circle and tweak my nipples until they're hard and aching. He raises my arms, guiding my hands to the edge of the shower wall where I hold on as his hands slide back to my body. Skimming over my hips, holding me in place as he continues slowly grinding against my ass. I want to arch my back, I want him to push all that heat inside of me, but he holds me firm.

When I'm ready to whimper with need, one of his hands slides lower. My hips jerk as his fingers begin to circle, his skin rough enough to produce a delicious friction. Heat begins building in my belly immediately, he gets impossibly harder against my ass, and then his fingers flutter away.

A groan slides past my lips and I let go of the wall with one hand to reach down and relieve some of the tension but his hand gently takes my wrist, pinning it to me. His breathing is ragged and we stand for a moment, pressed together. Shane reaches to the side and sets the soap on a shelf.

We rinse off, every flick of his fingers bringing a little shudder or jerk. He turns off the water, grabbing a thick towel and wrapping me in it. He wraps his arms around me over the towel, rubbing gently, and I feel his lips in my hair.

Shane steps away and lays another towel gently over my hair, I towel it dry and then wrap my hair up, turban style on my head. He's drying off as well, and then he straightens, wrapping the towel around his hips. The sight of him, water droplets still lingering on his chest, trickling down to the edge of his towel as he stares at me in the moonlight is almost enough to send me over the edge without another touch.

Opening the door to the house, Shane takes my hand and leads me to his bed.

Glow and Afterglow

S^{*hane*}

There's a little lamp on my dresser that's made out of a pink lump of salt. Judy insisted I have it on in there because it supposedly exudes healthy stuff into the air. I don't bother to argue with Judy much, it never really works, so there it sits.

I'm glad for it now, because I flip the little switch and it fills the room with a warm glow. I turn to Nica and reach for the towel on her head, unwrapping it carefully and tossing it on a basket in the corner. Her long dark hair tumbles down her shoulders, wet strands like spun silk clinging to her skin. Staring up at me through her lashes, she drops the other towel that's wrapped around her chest. It falls in a pool around her feet and her skin glows golden in the dim light.

I drop my own towel, and while the walk into the house gave me a minute to get myself under control, my dick has other ideas and it's straining toward Nica like it's a compass and she's true north. *It's been a long damn time.* She smiles, stepping close to me, turning her face up for a kiss as she presses her belly into my hips. The feel of her is intoxicating, I cup her face in my hands, kissing her long and slow, licking along the seam of her lips as they part for me.

Her hands flutter along my ribs, tracing the muscles and finding my nipples, hard little points that she gives a tiny pinch before moving on. She reaches around and grabs my ass, pulling me with her as she backs up a couple of steps. She pulls away, sitting on the edge of the bed, and looks up at me as she spreads her legs wide, pulling me close to stand between her knees.

Football, cold showers, getting kicked by a mad heifer, anything I can think of to keep from exploding as I feel her tongue and I'm almost undone.

I take a quick step back and she gasps as I scoop a hand under her knees, my other arm behind her back, lift, and toss her up to the head of the bed. She laughs breathlessly as I join her, my hips pushing her legs apart, kissing her hungrily. I will never get enough of her soft lips molding to mine, the noises she makes, the little sighs as I kiss my way down her neck, grazing her collarbone with my teeth to make her moan. Finding her nipple, I suck it in and worry it carefully with my teeth, she gasps, thrusting against my mouth. I suck in hard again, letting go with a little pop noise that makes her gasp and giggle as I kiss my way down her belly.

I feel her fingers winding into my hair. She whimpers as I lean down and lay a kiss on the inside of each of her thighs before returning. I lick lightly, the barest of touches, before sucking it in hard. She lets out a hard moan, hips bucking against my face.

"Get up here," she gasps, "oh Shane, now, I want to feel you inside of me."

Giving her one more good suck, I raise my weight up on my arms and look at her. She's panting with need, her nails digging into my shoulders trying to pull me up the bed.

"Condom," I grit out, dying to drive into her, I want to feel her heat, make her scream.

"I have an IUD, it's okay," she gasps. My hips buck forward and I bury myself in one hard stroke with a groan. She sighs with pleasure and I start a slow rhythm, pushing deep. I feel her hips moving with me and her hands lock around my neck. Her eyes are shut, her head arched back, soft moans trickle from her lips in a steady stream.

I feel her moving faster, starting to look for her release. Sliding a hand under her back, I pull her tight against my body and flip us so that I'm sitting up against the headboard and she's riding me. She immediately starts moving her hips, keeping me deep inside her, forward, back, forward, back. The movement is hypnotizing, I put my hands on her hips, one thumb sliding down to add friction at her center.

Nica gasps, looking down at me, and moves faster. When I feel her start to lose her rhythm, her movements becoming jerky, I grab her hips and move my own. She throws her head back, I feel her muscles flutter and squeeze hard, she screams my name, sending me over the edge.

Nica's hands find my chest, pressing hard as she slowly stops moving, riding the aftershocks. I reach up and hug her to me, scooting us down the bed, and pulling her in close. I feel her lips, feather-light, kissing my chest and the base of my neck, and then she snuggles in and I feel her body relax.

My brain wants to keep me awake, worrying about the future and where this leads, because I don't see any road but one. I shove it all away, determined to take what she can give, and go to sleep.

Bedhead and Coffee

❦

Nica

I stare at the unfamiliar ceiling for a moment when I wake up, and then Shane's arm tightens around me and I feel his lips press into my hair. *Not a dream, thank god.* Tilting my head back to look at him, he smiles and leans down to press a soft kiss to my lips and squeezes me in one more time before rolling away and sliding his arm out from under me. Tossing the covers back, he gets up and pads across the room to the attached bathroom and I hear him brushing his teeth.

"Coffee?" he returns to the bedroom in boxers, grabbing a pair of jeans off the chair and pulling them on. *In a perfect world, Shane would walk around at all times wearing only a pair of jeans. Or nothing at all, nothing would also be acceptable.* He grins at me and I panic for a second thinking I said all that out loud. I didn't, but I'm pretty sure he can tell what I'm thinking anyway.

"Yes please, that would be wonderful," I'll just be glad to have a minute, I need to go eat some of his toothpaste, and my hair is an epic disaster. It's been washed, not combed, and sexed… my best bet at this point is probably a hat. I'm also going to have to borrow some clothes…this was obviously not a planned seduction.

Shane gives me another grin, my vagina springs to life and starts catcalling, and it's all I can do not to tackle him and drag him back to bed. I hear him thumping down the stairs and I hop out of bed and head for the bathroom.

Ten minutes later, feeling mildly presentable, *except for my hair, I had to roll it in a bun and secure it with a pencil, I look like a librarian that just had a lot of sex,* I head down the stairs myself. Shane meets me at the bottom with a cup of coffee, waving a hand at milk and sugar on the kitchen table. I tuck one leg under me as I sit on one of the chairs at the table, both hands around the mug, appreciating the heat in the light chill of the morning.

"Well… that's hot," he rumbles softly, and I glance at my coffee, confused, until I catch Shane's eyes as they run appreciatively up my leg, taking in the boxers I've rolled at the waist to make them fit and the denim shirt I stole from the closet. I get a flash of heat in my chest that blooms on my cheeks, and I smile as I sip my coffee, glancing at him over the rim. He waits until I'm done, crosses the room to me, and holds out his hand. Taking it, he pulls me up out of the chair and into his arms, kissing me breathless. *Oh yessssss.*

F**k Yeah I Can

*S*hane

Pulling up to the curb, it almost hurts to let Nica get out of my truck. I want her to pull me inside, I want her to take me to her bed. She lingers for a moment, playing with my fingers laced through hers, and then laughs quietly.

"I'd really like to drag you inside," she whispers, laughing again when I groan. "I'll see you in a few hours." She smiles, leaning over to brush a kiss across my lips. She's being smart, she's the one who reminded me Katie will be home later this morning. Nica, sitting at the kitchen table, sipping coffee, *wearing my clothes*, might not be the best way to broach the subject that we're together with Katie.

I get out of the truck, walking around to her side, she slides an arm around my waist and we walk to her door together. She unlocks the door, leaning up to kiss me again. Looking up at me her brown eyes sparkle with humor.

"Just for the record, not just any 'country boy' would have made my bucket list," she's smiling broadly now, eyes dancing, "if I ever did make such a list, I'd write 'sleep with Shane Tyler' as item number one, just so I could start making tally marks behind it." She spins away from me, laughing as I make a grab for her, surprised laughter bursting out of me. I settle for swatting her ass as she darts through the door, a satisfying little smack, and she jumps, glancing over her shoulder, her gaze challenging.

"*Surely* you can do better than that, Shane." My mouth goes dry and my dick about rips a hole in my jeans. *Fuck yeah I can.* Her gaze holds mine as she walks in and heads up the stairs, leaving the door open. I pause for a split second, watching her ass sway as she walks up the stairs and then I follow her. *Fuck yeah I can.*

I reach the top of the stairs and she's dropped the boxers on the floor, kicking them off. Unbuttoning the shirt, she lets that slide to the floor as well. With a wink, she turns and crawls onto the bed on all fours, her ass waving enticingly in the air. Shoving off my own jeans, I walk up behind her and take hold of her hips. I slowly push into her, savoring the feel of her stretching around me until she gasps and shoves backwards, driving me deep. I stroke her ass again and then give it a playful spank. Her reaction is perfect, she gives a little gasp and glances over her shoulder smiling.

Pumping in and out of her, I smack her ass again, a little harder now, settling into a rhythm, and every time my hand makes contact, her muscles contract around me and she sighs, 'yes'.

Never in a million years would I hurt her. I had a friend once who talked about his woman liking to be spanked. It seemed crazy until he said she explained that it heightens the sensation, makes what she's feeling almost overwhelming. *Fuck yeah I can.*

Her hips are slamming back into me and she's speeding up, close to coming, her ass is pink and warm under my hands. I change the angle and shorten my strokes, and when she shrieks my name I let go, pounding her hard through her climax, following with my own, her name on my lips. *Fuck yeah I can.*

So... Here's the Thing

*N*ica

Lying here tangled in the sheets, Shane's arms tight around me, I'm happier than I've ever been. He stirs, leaning his head down to kiss my shoulder softly.

"You awake?" His voice rumbles my ear through his chest, and I roll over to face him, propping my chin in my hands. *Okay, deep breath, now is a good time to tell him I'm not leaving, now is a good time to find out if he's really into me as a forever. Time to find out if he's my one.*

When Shane started yelling the other night, I suddenly understood that he was afraid, and it made sense. His fears were my own. I didn't want to hurt him. I didn't want to connect with Katie and then leave. I didn't want to walk away again. *I don't want to be alone anymore.*

"I have something to tell you," my voice is nervous. His eyes meet mine, steady and comforting. I take a deep breath and then the words tumble out.

"I'm buying the McGregor building downtown, it's going to house office space for the Organics line...and be the acting headquarters for a new cosmetics line I want to build." *I haven't slid that part by Evelyn yet, I don't want to be just her marketing flunky, I want to start something that is mine, and either she'll love it or...no, fuck that, she'll learn to love it.*

He sits up in the bed looking down at me, his face serious. I sit up too, on my knees, and then realize I feel too vulnerable, telling him all this naked. *Why isn't he saying anything?* Leaning over the edge of the bed, I grab a t-shirt hanging off the corner of the nightstand and pull it over my head.

As my head pops out the neck hole in a tangle of my hair, his hands are on me. Smoothing my hair back from my face, his lips crash into mine. He doesn't need to say anything. I smile against his lips and kiss him back, hard. I get it.

Everyone Else Saw It

*S*hane

Nica is staying.

Here in Gravity.

Nica is staying here in Gravity.

I barely remember the ride home, parking the truck in the lane.
I hop out, stopping to pet Barney as I walk toward the house.
Carl appears, leaving the house and we meet on the porch.

"You look like a man with a lot on his mind," Carl knows me
well.

"Nica and I are together." *Jesus take the wheel, I wasn't planning
to say that.* Carl pauses, startled, then his eyes crinkle and his
cheeks stretch in a big grin.

"…'bout time, Boss," he chuckles and continues on past me,
"'bout damn time." It makes my chest feel lighter to tell someone.
Makes it more real. She's staying. She wants to be here. *I might*

be able to keep her.

Heading on into the kitchen, Judy and Katie are busy building a small mountain of sandwiches to take out to the guys doing chores today. I don't run a big crew on the weekends, just enough to take care of the live stock.

"Morning, ladies," I tip a fake hat and swipe a sandwich, Judy smiles, wrapping up the tray.

"I'll just take these on out, the lemonade is already loaded up, don't want it getting warm." She pats me on the shoulder and then grabs the tray and heads outside.

"Hey Dad," Katie moves to sit at the table and starts polishing off her own sandwich. I drop a kiss on her head and take a seat across from her.

"Hey kiddo, how was the Spanish thing?" She chews a minute before answering.

"It was fine, Josh and Hannah spent the whole trip making out. It was so annoying that the teacher had to split them up. Elena dropped her phone and it fell through the sewer grate… that's about it." She takes another bite.

"I'm dating Nica." *WHAT IS WRONG WITH ME. I can't shut my damn mouth to save my life.* Katie swallows her bite of sandwich and then glances at me, grinning.

"Cool… Don't screw it up, *especially* not before prom," she giggles and heads upstairs, leaving me staring after her. *How could everyone see this but me.*

Glancing at the clock, I have about an hour before I go pick Nica up for Sunday afternoon dinner. Heading upstairs, I grab a quick shower, pulling on jeans and a t-shirt. Walking over to the bed, I grab my phone. Two missed calls and a cryptic text from Nica.

Nica: Call me, it's important, and meet me downtown. Bring Katie.

What the hell? I call her number and she answers immediately.

"Shane, I have to cancel on dinner, something's come up." She sounds out of breath and in a hurry.

"What's going on, Nica?" My heart squeezes.

"Nothing bad, I promise, can you bring Katie to the new building? I want to show you something." She waits to hear me agree and then disconnects.

Well...that was weird. I text Aunt Sheila not to expect me this week. I holler to Katie and she appears a few minutes later, she changed her clothes quick and washed her face.

"What's going on, Dad?"

"No idea, Nica wants us to meet her downtown, she wants to show us something." I don't know if she wants us to see the building? It doesn't seem like her to be so anxious she'd cancel plans just to have a walk through...must be something else. Katie chatters away unconcerned through the drive, we pull up next to the building and Nica is waiting there, smiling.

"Hi Katie, good trip?" Her voice is brimming with excitement. Katie is caught up in it right away.

"Yeah it was super-fun, what's going on? Is there a surprise?" She's bouncing on her toes and Nica laughs.

"There is," she turns to me, "sorry I had to change things up last minute," she leans in and murmurs, "as much as I would like to see Wayne in his natural habitat and meet Myrna...this couldn't wait." I shake my head smiling.

"There'll be other weekends, what's going on?" She nods and reaches out a hand to Katie.

"So after I saw you the other day, I spoke to my friend Mimsy," she grins as Katie lets out a giggle, "she has a fondness for mimosas," Nica laughs. "Anyway," Nica continues, "the thing you have to understand about Mimsy is that she never does anything unless she does it *big*...so when I asked her about some dresses for you to look at for prom, she sent them." Katie squeals and starts looking around, glancing in the front windows.

"Mimsy's husband is a designer named Jonathon Christopher," Nica barely gets the words out before Katie squeals louder.

"OMG I've heard of him, I've heard of him, OMG, OMG, OMG!" Katie is dancing in place on the sidewalk, yanking on Nica's hand excitedly.

"Katie you're going to pull her arm off," I put a hand on Katie's shoulder to settle her down. Katie blushes and lets go of Nica.

"Sorry! This is just very cool, I'll be good now, promise." She solemnly crosses her heart. Nica is smiling broadly, enjoying Katie's reaction.

"You're fine honey, let's go in and take a look." Nica opens the doors with a flourish and a smile and ushers Katie and I inside. I let out a low whistle, this place has some great character. The floors are clean, and in the center is a large three-way mirror like you'd see in a dressing room. There are two chairs arranged as if for a very small audience. Wren and a man, *I think it's a man, I could be wrong, he's wearing makeup and heels, whatever,* are standing near the mirror.

Mimsy Nails It

⚜

Nica

"Ohhh! Wren my little minx you weren't joking! She is a petite little niblet! Sweetie! Come closer, let me *look* at you!" Julian's voice is full of drama, he practically sings the words. Katie is immediately enthralled, she skips across the room and lets him take her hands as if they've been friends for years.

When I asked Mimsy to ship me some prom dresses, I should have known it wouldn't be simple. She put a rack of dresses, all the shoes and accessories and *Jonathon's assistant* on a private plane. Julian called shortly after Shane left me this morning to tell me he would be arriving soon. It was a mad scramble to get the space opened and cleaned, but Wren dropped everything and helped me make the calls and we got it done.

I stay back with Shane, letting this be Katie's moment. Leaning close, I bump my shoulder into his and he slides an

116

arm around my waist. *Oh, public affection already? I like it, but...* As if sensing the question, he leans down and whispers in my ear.

"I told Katie we're together." A warm glow blooms in my chest as I glance up at him. Together. I like that very much. Slipping my arm around his waist, we walk over and I introduce him to Julian. Katie's eyes are as big as saucers when she finds out who he is, Wren gives her a squeeze.

"Wait until you see what he brought, Katie, I helped him take them all out of their special bags!" Wren is caught up in the magic as well, she's practically clapping her hands with excitement.

"Tut-tut-tut, my little pipska don't spoil the surprise!" Julian admonishes with a teasing finger wag, herding Shane and I over to the chairs. "Give us a few moments and then we will put on a show for you!" Julian air-kisses us both, *Shane's face is absolutely priceless*, and darts behind the mirrors.

Katie lets out an astonished shriek at the sight of all the dresses. I had a quick glance myself and I could see that Mimsy chose well, every color, every cut, every fabric would make Katie the belle of the ball. Now she just has to choose her favorite.

Sitting back in my chair during this moment of relative peace, Shane reaches over and links his fingers through mine, lifting our hands up to brush a kiss across my knuckles.

"Darlin', you're amazin'," he says quietly, "Katie is very lucky to have your help." I smile and then look toward the mirrors, waiting for the first dress. I don't have the words, nor the inclination, to tell him that I want Katie to have what I didn't.

There's no question that I've always had money, we've got *loads* of money. What I didn't have was someone who cared enough to come along and help me find the perfect dress for my school dances. I had an endless bankroll but I was essentially alone. I spent my shopping trips with people who were paid to care or friends who pretended to…it was a lonely way to grow up.

Mentally giving myself a shake, I squeeze Shane's hand lightly and then turn to watch his face as Katie walks around the mirrors in the first dress. I've seen the dresses and I know she will look amazing. The first thing I want to see is his face when he sees her, *and it is everything.* His jaw clenches and then he can't stop smiling at her, his eyes are shiny but only I can tell.

Turning to look myself, Katie is beaming in a pink dress with a gold overlay. The top is a princess neckline with broad straps, the bottom is a gold and pink cloud. Her hair has been pulled up in a twist with gold clips and she's wearing a gold necklace with a single large pink crystal drop.

"She is perfection, and it's only the first dress," I can't stop smiling either. Julian comes out and fusses with the dress a little bit and then has Katie do a full spin.

"It's lovely darling, let's file that away in our little mind gallery and try on the next one, shall we?" Julian trills. Katie nods, spinning one more time and he whisks her back behind the mirrors.

A few minutes later, Katie is back, this time in sky blue edged with a thick band of crystals, it's a long slim skirt and a cropped top, sleeveless with a high neck. This is followed by a violet number with a slinky back that makes Shane's jaw creak, I give Julian a discreet head shake on that one. Next is a dark pink with slashes of something iridescent worked through the skirt.

Each one is as beautiful as the last, the jewelry perfect, and Katie is beside herself, smiling and blushing and chatting with

Julian. I hear a gasp from Wren as she helps Katie into the next dress, and Julian murmurs something excitedly. Shane and I watch intently, waiting for her to come out.

"Honey, I think you've found it," Shane's voice is rough as Katie practically floats out to stand in front of the mirrors. Staring at herself for a moment, Katie turns to us, eyes shining.

"Dad, Nica, I love this," her voice is high and excited. She is a vision. Julian comes up behind her to straighten and fuss, he's smiling too, and for the first time all afternoon, has nothing to say.

A collar of sapphire crystals circles her neck, making her already beautiful blue eyes enormous and striking. Diaphanous material is carefully gathered at the collar to form a panel on Katie's chest and at the back, dropping sheer to the floor, leaving her beautiful arms bare.

The diaphanous material starts as a dark sapphire blue, mirroring the collar that anchors it at her neck but starting at her hips it is covered in the most delicate beadwork that morphs from blue through all the shades of blues and greens until it ends with a hem of emerald crystals. The underlay dress is brushed silk in dark teal, perfectly setting off the sapphire and emerald accents of the overlay. It is cut simply, a straight edged bust with very thin straps. It fits her form as if it were made to her exact measurements, just brushing the floor, a center slit stops at her knees making it easy for her to walk. The dress is too intricate to need a necklace, but Julian has put Katie in earrings that are each one long strand of sapphire crystals, almost brushing her shoulders. They sparkle and gleam in the light.

The room has gone quiet, all of us staring at Katie in her perfect dress. Finally, Katie herself breaks the silence.

"This is going to be the *best prom ever,*" she whispers.

That's That

‿◦❀◦‿

Shane

Julian does some puttering around, pins a couple things here and there, and then has Katie slide the dress off. She gets back into her regular clothes and she and Wren ooh and aah over the dresses a little more while Julian gets busy making the one she chose perfect.

It doesn't seem to take him any time at all and then he's carefully tucking the dress into a garment bag and handing Katie a shoebox with her fancy shoes and a smaller box with the earrings. He makes a quick phone call and, like magic, a couple of big guys pull up in a black SUV, load up all the dresses, shoes and jewelry carefully.

Julian gives hugs and air-kisses all around, earnestly encourages Wren to consider coming to the city to be his intern, "I'll steal you away darling, just you wait!" Wren is flattered beyond words, she can't stop smiling. With one last hug for Nica, Julian whirls out the door.

Nica and I sit back down in the chairs, happy and quiet, Katie sprawls out on the floor, hands behind her head, looking up at the ceiling. Of course, being a teenager, she's quiet for about three seconds.

"I am just so happy right now." Her voice is bubbling with glee, I can see her making plans, mentally figuring out her hair and nail polish, and all that other stuff. Then she gasps and glances at Nica.

"Oh-my-gosh, I've got to call Miles, I bet we can still change the flowers to something really cool, I bet they haven't made them yet, I'll be right back!" She's up off the floor and heads out the front door for some privacy. We see her excitedly talking into her phone, gesturing and laughing, some of the movements are unmistakably Julian. Nica and I laugh watching her and then we look at each other, smiling.

"I don't know what I can say to get across what I'm feeling, but I'll start with 'thank you.'" It's hard to put into words what it means when someone treats your kid as if they are important and special. Nica does.

"I'm getting awfully attached to her," Nica says quietly sliding a glance at me and then looking down at her hands, "I guess it's a good thing I'm putting down some roots." My heart stutters and then starts beating a little harder. I've worked hard for everything I've ever had, my entire life. To have someone like Nica practically fall out of the sky into my lap feels like too much luck.

"Yeah, about that, how'd your family react?" I wait for her to glance at me again and make eye contact, I want this to be real, I want to believe in us.

"Oh…well, I'll tell them when I've got all the details wrapped up." she keeps her voice light and casual, but then she looks at me and stands up walking a few steps away, turning to stare hard at me and I hear the tiny little wobble in her voice that tells me she's worried. "My mother hates anything she can't control, so I'll have to do some selling on the finer points of my plan, but it'll be fine. I'm a big girl, *well* past leaving the nest."

I hold out my hands and she walks back to me, letting me pull her into my lap. We sit together a while, watching Katie through the window. Finally I clear my throat a tiny bit and she shifts to look at me.

"Doesn't matter what your mom thinks, I'm keeping you... I love you city girl." Nica's lips part and her eyes shine, she needed to hear it, I'm glad I wasn't too stupid to say it.

"Well I love you too, country boy, so I guess that's that." Her voice is soft and happy, she relaxes against me again, and I hold her close.

Back to the City

※ ❧ ❧ ※

Nica

The next week is a blur. The building is officially signed over to me and work has begun. I've been putting insane hours into the plan for the new cosmetics line I want to launch, the pitch has to be perfect, Evelyn is a hard sell. I have also begun the process of letting them know I would like to stay in Gravity indefinitely.

The first step was telling Tara to have the rental car picked up. The second was flying home for a few days to select more of my things to have shipped to Gravity. I arrived back in the city this morning. A driver took me to my parent's home, I arrived just before lunch was served.

"VeeVee dear, it's good to see you home," my mother sounds sincere and I walk to her side for a brief hug. She's dining alone, my father lunches with his racquetball partner at the club every Tuesday. Walking to my seat, the staff hastily set another place.

"Thank you Mother, it's just for a short visit, I'm going to have some more of my things shipped to Gravity, and I wanted to go over a few things with you in person." I begin eating, waiting for her response.

"Certainly darling, how are you liking that quaint little farm town?" I don't care for her tone, she says 'quaint little farm town' like the words are an insult, but I swallow my indignation. I realize she's saying exactly what I would have before I went to Gravity. I decide it's time for a rare show of honesty, all cards on the table.

"I'm going to stay in Georgia long-term," I pause, not looking away and take a deep breath. "I'm in love with Shane Tyler as well." I hold up a hand so she'll let me finish, "I don't want to cheapen it by saying I'm staying for him, I decided to stay in Gravity before I knew he felt the same way about me."

Evelyn carefully finishes chewing and dabs a napkin to the corners of her lips before responding.

"I see...so I send you to the country, hoping you'll grow up and find yourself, and you start sleeping with the help?"

My mouth flies open, an angry retort on my lips, until I look at her face and see that she's smiling mischievously.

"I'm joking Veevee," she puts up a mollifying hand and continues, "Mimsy was gushing over her charitable act with the girl's prom dress after a few too many drinks at the country club the other night. She's missing you by the way. Anyway, she said that Julian reported you and Mr. Tyler were very chummy." My mother is like a cat that got in the cream, so satisfied with her little spy network.

"...And speaking of charitable acts, Martin called about some paperwork he needs you to sign for something involving a scholarship fund? You *have* been busy, haven't you darling?"

Evelyn waves for her plate to be taken away and a small cup of sorbet is placed in front of her, she carefully dips a spoon in, taking a contemplative bite. I'm silent, I don't know where she's going with this, better to wait. Her next words surprise me.

"Are you happy Veevee?" Evelyn asks softly, and her tone makes me stop and answer her for real, without the usual veneer of sophistication and coolness that my mother and I have allowed to shape our relationship.

"I am, Mother, truly. It's hard to put into words, but that's where I need to be, it just feels right." I want her to understand what I'm not saying, and to my surprise, she stares at me for a moment and then nods as if she does.

"I'm happy for you darling, all your father and I wanted was for you to find yourself and develop a sense of purpose. I'd say you've done *far* more than we expected." She smiles and resumes her dessert, conversation over. I feel warm all over. That was, from Evelyn, akin to declaring her love and support from the highest mountain for all to hear. I'll take it. I pick up my spoon.

Girls Night Out

∼❧∼

*N*ica

Word travels fast that I've made an impromptu visit to the city, and it isn't long before the girls are blowing up my phone. I'd hoped to avoid a night of clubbing, but it doesn't appear that I will be able to when I get Mimsy's final texts threatening violence if I don't get ready immediately. Standing in my closet, I look around at all of the beautiful clothes, and picture Shane's face. *What a field day he would have teasing me about the sheer abundance, my closet here is bigger than my living room back in Gravity.* Katie would have even *more* fun trying on every dress.

Now that I'm back in the city, the sweet little family of two seems very far away. I've only been gone for a day, and I'm surprised at how much I miss them. That thought quickly morphs into wondering if they miss me…and then wondering why they would. *The life they have in Georgia doesn't change one bit if I'm not there...what if Shane decides I'm not worth the trouble...*

I'm still standing in my closet, now miserable, when my phone starts buzzing.

"Get down here V! We're waiting!" Mimsy shrieks before disconnecting. *Some things never change.* Quickly throwing on a short black dress and some glittery heels, I grab a purse and head for the door. *Maybe a night out with the girls is just what I need.*

Mims and Jillian, my two best friends are waiting in the back of a sleek black car. Mims pops the cork on a bottle of champagne as I get in the car.

"To V's return from country hell!" Mims trills, taking a long drink and passing the bottle to me. Taking a sip and passing it along, I try to get into the spirit of a fun night out. *There's a handsome devil in the country...*

I'm saved from talking about my trip and life in the country by the fact that neither of the other women actually care where I've been or what I've been doing for two months. They instantly start trying to catch me up on the latest, who's been sleeping around, who's wearing what, who made best dressed last week... Smiling along, I laugh in all the right places, but I feel like I'm looking at my friends with new eyes. *Have we always been this shallow? Yes...of course we have.*

Arriving at Eli's, we smile at the line of hopefuls we're passing and the velvet rope clicks back into place behind us.

"Head for the lounge girls! I'm going to go talk to Simone a mo', heard she broke up with Alphonse...wouldn't *that* be a shame!" Jillian sweeps off into the crowd before we can answer, a predatory smile stretching her lips. I shake my head and let Mims drag me through the crowd to the private area in the back.

"The piranhas smell blood, look out," Mimsy murmurs as we settle into one of the circular booths. Right on cue, several beautiful people peel off from the bar and head in our direction.

"V is that you?! I heard you were in rehab darling, you look fantastic!"

"Oh my god, your hair, who has been touching your hair! Have you been cheating on Antonio? He's not going to like that babes!"

"What is she wearing?"

The obnoxious voices wash over me, mingling with the whispers and the beat of the music. I grab the bottle from Mimsy and take a long drink. *It's like I never left.* As each of them get bored and wander away, they are replaced with a never-ending lineup of people wanting a piece of me. Keeping a cool smile plastered on my face, I engage in mindless chatter and find myself longing for the quiet of the country.

When I see Amberly, *who I loathe,* saunter away from the bar, a malicious gleam in her eye, I quickly excuse myself before I get roped into a conversation. Walking down the service hall for a moment of quiet, I stop and lean against the cool tile, and notice my phone buzzing insistently. It's not a number I recognize, but it's a Georgia area code. Curious, I answer.

"Nica?" His voice wraps around me like a warm blanket.

"Shane?" It's ridiculous how happy I am to hear his voice.

"Yeah, Darlin' it's me, had a little accident with my phone, I don't really want to talk ab-"

"He dropped it in fresh cow poop!" Katie pipes over the line in the background, followed by gales of laughter. I hear Shane unsuccessfully trying to shush Katie.

"Then he couldn't even pick it up because he startled the cow and she *stepped on it!*" Katie squawks quickly, her voice getting louder and then quieter as if she's dodging around the room, followed by more squeals of laughter.

"Thanks kid," Shane's voice is full of amused embarrassment, "you're so helpful. Now go on, I'll bring you your phone in a minute." After a few more seconds of laughing, the connection gets quiet.

"You still there?" Shane's voice is lower now, that slow sexy drawl caressing my skin as if he were actually with me.

"I'm here…and I'm glad you called, I miss you a little bit." I'm glad he can't see the blush creeping up my cheeks. I'm not good with voicing feelings.

"I miss you more than a little bit, Darlin'…figured I'd call, just wanted to hear your voice…" he laughs quietly, "also I was getting too far in my own head a little while ago…started worrying that you'd get back to the city and remember how much you love it…maybe more than some hick from the country."

My heart squeezes hard and I feel warm all over. He's missing me too, I'm not being crazy.

"I don't know about some hick," I'm sure he can hear the smile in my voice, "but there's a handsome farmer that has caught my eye."

"Uh-oh darlin' you'll have to tell me who that lucky man is so I can kick his ass and steal you for my own," he chuckles. "You having a good time? Gettin' all caught up with your friends?"

"Oh, yes, it's been…great!" I force a cheerful tone. I'm not sure what's wrong with me, this night is just like every other night out with my friends since I can remember.

"I'm glad to hear it, I'll let you get back to them, I just wanted to tell you I don't have a phone 'til I get in tomorrow for a new one," Shane pauses, "you can use this number if you want to, but you'll have to talk to Katie first." His smooth, deep voice is full of amusement.

"I'm glad you called Shane," there's a lot of things I'd like to say to him, but I just wait.

"I'll see you in a few days darlin," his words shiver across my skin and I clutch the phone hard to my ear.

"I'll see you in a few days," I whisper back. Disconnecting I put the phone in my clutch and head back out into the noise.

Sunrise Blessing

*N*ica

The party goes on and on, a blur of noise and dancing and laughter ending with an after-party at Mimsy's. We watch the sun come up as we lounge on a huge floatie in her pool drinking mimosas. Polishing hers off, Mimsy tosses the glass in the pool, ignoring the long-suffering sigh of her butler who retrieves it with a net.

"You're different, V." She announces without looking at me, beckoning to the butler to mix her another mimosa.

"How so?" I ask, curious, holding out my own glass, but waiting for the net rather than dropping it into the pool. *See, she's right...a month ago I would have tossed the glass in the pool and let him pick up after me.*

"I don't know, can't put my finger on it," Mimsy lazily boops me on the nose, "but you seem...maybe happier? I don't know, all glow-y?" She hiccups and her eyes get wide, finding mine in a comical drunken panic. "Ohmygod you're preggers aren't you, ohmygod!" She attempts to sit up and look at me better, upending the floatie and we both land in the pool with a shriek.

"No I am not *preggers* you bitch, don't you dare start spreading *that* around," I sputter with laughter as we find our footing, making our way to the steps at the end of the pool. Shivering in the chill morning air, Mimsy giggles helplessly, holding out her hands for me to pull her up the stairs.

"Trevor turn on the jets," she calls, shimmying out of her dress and heading for the hot tub in her bra and thong. I follow suit, leaving my black dress in a little pile. We sink happily into the warmth as the bubbles circle. Trevor brings us two more mimosas and she fixes me with a tipsy stare.

"So what is it V? Julian told me you were pretty chummy with that farmer, Dave? Dane?"

"Shane," I correct her quietly, "and yes, we are *chummy*." Sipping my mimosa I wait for her reaction.

"So…go slumming in the country, pick up a hot muscle-y farmer for a roll in the hay?" She toasts me with her already-empty glass, "good for you babe! Get some!" Lifting her glass to her lips she tips it up, almost falling over until she realizes it's empty. Setting it on the side, she lets loose a small burp.

"That's not quite the way this went, Mims," miraculously I retain my calm, honestly if our roles were reversed I would have made the same assumption and been just as crass. "I'm staying there."

"Where?" Mimsy looks at me blearily, waving for another mimosa.

"This is just a visit, Mims, I'm setting up a residence in Georgia, I'm going to see where things go with Shane." I pause, and then wait a moment, and I'm starting to wonder if she fell asleep with her eyes open, *again*, when she burps again softly. Reaching to take her next mimosa she sighs.

"Huh…so not just a fling? Well…okay." She says simply, raising her glass in a toast. "To you and your country boy."

Make An Entrance

*S*hane

Nica has been gone for four days. It's quiet here without her presence. She's due back later this morning, she promised Katie she would help her get all ready for prom tonight. I'm outside, avoiding Katie and all her nervous energy, helping Carl fix a belt on the truck.

A fancy sport utility pulls up the lane, kind of a dark gray with tinted windows. It slows and stops near the truck and Nica hops out, smiling.

"New wheels?" I wipe my hands on a rag and meet her halfway, putting my arms around her waist and lifting her in a hug.

"It didn't seem worth it to keep a rental at this point," she smiles as her hands grab my shoulders and slide up to my jaw and she kisses me. Slowly setting her back on her feet, she links her arm through mine as we walk toward the house.

"How was the city?" *I hope it was boring.*

"Oh," she sighs, glancing at me, "Honestly? It was exactly the same, lunch at the club with Daddy, drinks with Mimsy, plus I spent a lot of time going through the things I wanted to have sent here and going over the recent numbers with Mother..." she pauses, thinking.

"It was fine, it was good to see everyone, I think maybe *I'm* the thing that has changed. Somehow all the things that used to be so important, events, clubs, all of those things just seem kind of senseless now. They just didn't mean as much when I thought of what I want to build here." She tapers off, her eyes sliding away from mine, embarrassed. *I swear she should be able to hear my heart right now, the fucking thing just burst into song.*

I don't know how to respond to that, so I back her into the wall of the house and kiss the daylights out of those beautiful lips. A few minutes later, I walk her into the house and Katie immediately comes flying down the stairs.

"Nica, you made it!" Katie drags Nica back upstairs, both of them laughing and I head back outside, knowing when I'm in the way. A few hours later, I hear Nica calling me from the porch. As I walk across the lawn, the sun catches her hair just right and she glows.

"Hey, she's ready except for putting her dress on and Miles will be here in about a half hour, so I figured maybe you would want to get cleaned up?" She looks pointedly at the shower.

"Yeah, you're probably right, we should probably take some pictures, huh?" I look at her just in time to see the expected eye roll followed by a sassy grin.

"Yes, of course, I might have gone a little overboard and asked my film guy to bring his camera out for a few pictures..." *Of course she did.* "After all, you only do this once...well twice since she'll be a senior next year I guess…well shit, you get the sentiment," she gives an exasperated laugh.

Walking over to the shower, I duck behind the screen, just in case any of the men or Katie wander by, and get undressed. Turning on the water I start to wash my hair and get cleaned up and when I turn to rinse I see she's still standing there. Her eyes are dark with lust and I'm about to drag her in with me. As we stare at each other, breath coming faster, we realize at the same moment that now is most definitely not the time.

"That is too hot for words," Nica gasps, practically throwing herself through the door going into the house.

I'm showered and dressed in clean jeans and a button down shirt when Miles arrives. He's a good looking kid, a few inches shorter than me but quite a bit taller than Katie, he's got a black tux on and he's clutching a plastic box with the flowers in it. I let him in the house to sit on the couch a minute and head for the bottom of the stairs to holler at Katie.

As I open my mouth, Nica appears and just points a finger at me to shut up, I choke back a laugh. She walks down the stairs and says hello to Miles, telling him Katie will just be a minute.

While he fidgets nervously, I step close to Nica and murmur in her ear.

"You've been up there for hours, what the heck is left to do?"

"Make an entrance," she breathes back and then I look up the stairs and there's my Katie.

Katie looks so beautiful it's all I can do not to shove her back in her room and never let her grow up. She's beaming, she knows she looks good. Nica has put her hair up in a big crown on her head with curls and braids and little gems twinkling here and there.

She lifts the hem of her dress with one hand and she's carrying her strappy sandals hooked over a finger. I see that and laugh, she sees where I'm looking and she laughs too.

"Didn't want to ruin the whole night with a busted leg," she giggles, walking carefully down the stairs and straight over to where Miles is standing. He looks like someone hit him in the face with a shovel, but he shakes it off and holds out the box of flowers.

"You look beautiful," he says, kind of quiet like he's hoping I won't hear, "here, hold this and give me your shoes." Katie's eyes widen a little bit as she holds out the sandals and damn if the kid doesn't take a knee and hold the shoe while she slips her foot in. He carefully does the little buckle and then helps her with the other one. Katie's cheeks pink up and she ducks her head a tiny bit.

"Thanks, Miles, you look really good too." Katie opens the box, exclaiming over the flowers.

"Wow, I was hoping you could get them changed but I wasn't expecting anything *this* good!" She pulls out the boutonniere, it's a dark pinky-purple rose with little dark violet flowers next to it. Katie hands the box back to Miles to hold as she pins the flower on his jacket carefully. When she's done, he opens the box again and takes her flowers out.

"Um, the lady at the flower shop said she got this arm thing in special, she showed me a picture," Miles is blushing with all eyes on him, but he only has eyes for Katie. He touches the upper part of her arm and holds out the flower.

"Oh that is sooooooo pretty, Miles you killed this," Katie breathes, holding out her arm and letting him slide it up a few inches above her elbow. It's a delicate wire cuff with the flowers anchored in the middle of the swirl, roses and other flowers I can't name and that little violet stuff and some sparkly things.

It's over the top amazing and I have a sneaky suspicion this is Nica at work again.

Nica is studiously avoiding my gaze, so I put an arm around her shoulder and drop a quick kiss in her hair near her ear.

"You're amazing, you know that?" I whisper, and her cheeks pink up just a little. *Yep, knew it, she upgraded the flowers too.* The guy from Nica's film crew is discreetly clicking away from the other side of the room, and after the flowers are done, we head outside. He takes some more pictures of Katie and Miles and then some of me and Katie, I have him take a couple with Nica in them too, her smile says it all.

A Picnic

N^{ica}

We see the kids off, Katie is ecstatic, she can't wait to see all her friends, and Miles is obviously completely smitten. *It made my heart go pitter-pat when he put her shoes on her, so sweet.* There's a dinner, dance and then some sort of after-prom party that lasts through the night. Holding hands, we walk up to the house, Shane pauses and turns to me.

"Stay here a minute," he waits until I nod and then heads over to the shed. I hear the 4-wheeler roar to life. He drives across the yard, stopping near me. Hopping off the 4-wheeler, he heads into the house for a minute, returning with a covered basket. There's some kind of strap he uses to anchor the basket on the metal rack of the 4-wheeler.

"Want to go for a ride?" he gives me *that* grin, and oh yes, I want to go for a ride. *That kind of ride.*

"Oh yes sir," I giggle softly as I climb on behind him, wrapping my hands around his waist, I let my fingers explore his abs. I hear a little groan escape his lips and then he guns the 4-wheeler and we head out across the grass.

Shane takes a meandering path that eventually leads us near the river. He follows along the edge for a while and then stops in a grove of weeping willows. *This is like a movie set...of a really good romance, I swear if he pulls a blanket and a bottle of wine, no scratch that, it'll be beer, out of that basket...*

He waits for me to climb off and then he gets off too, unhooking the basket and flipping the lid open. His smile is confused when I laugh at the sight of a blanket, a six pack of beer and a pie. *Oh my god he's perfect.*

"You are *too* perfect," I reach out to take the blanket, stepping in close to kiss him first. Turning, I lay the blanket out on the soft grass under the trees.

Shane sets the beer and the basket with the pie still in it on a corner of the blanket. Kicking off his shoes, he walks on the blanket and sits down holding his arms out to me. I kick mine off too and sit between his legs, my back nestled to his stomach and open beers for both of us, passing him one. We drink in silence for a few minutes, watching the river flow by.

I rest my beer in the handle of the basket so it won't spill and turn sideways, coming up on my knees between his legs. His arm is braced behind him as he leans back, and his other hand is holding his beer. I take it from him and put it with mine. Turning back, I run my hands up his chest and start unbuttoning his shirt. He lets me without moving a muscle, when I reach the bottom button, I push his shirt off his shoulders, baring his chest, and he lifts one hand and then the other to shrug it off.

Tensing his abs, *swoon,* he sits up, his hands sliding around behind my thighs and he pulls one leg then the other over his so I'm straddling him. His hands slide around to hold my ass, and then my waist, and he tilts his head up and my lips find his. My hands are on his face and in his hair and I feel his slide inside my shirt. He pulls up the hem and we break the kiss long enough for him to pull it over my head.

Reaching behind me, he unfastens my bra and the early evening air raises goosebumps that he kisses away. I start to grind my hips against him, wishing there were no layers of clothing between us, moaning softly. My hair falls around us and he tilts his head back up, kissing me hard.

Hugging me to him, Shane flips us over so that my back is on the blanket. Unbuttoning my jeans he pulls them off and then stands and pushes his jeans and boxers off his hips. Sitting on the blanket beside me, he slides my underwear over my hips, leaning down and kissing my belly. Setting my clothes to the side, he lowers his weight over me, I wrap my legs around his waist and he groans. I feel him hard at my opening and then he pushes in, I feel a delicious stretch and he's kissing me again.

Pushing up through his arms, he starts a slow rhythm, thrusting at a perfect angle, his kisses full of heat. My nails are in his back, he pounds harder, and I arch my back, my head thrown back, as I feel the wave coming.

"Shane...Shane!" He keeps pounding, hitting that spot just right as I gasp his name over and over, climaxing hard.

Shane smiles down at me, still pumping his hips, but slower now, as I ride the aftershocks. He's still hard, and I push on his chest. He lifts up, sitting back, and I straddle his hips. Arms around his neck, I start moving my hips, forward and back until I feel him tense up. Finding my rhythm, I hold on to his shoulders while he leans back and braces his hands behind him on the blanket. Rocking my hips faster, I watch his face, his eyes are staring into mine, he's breathing hard until he leans forward fast, burying his head in my neck, his arms iron bands around my waist as he spasms into me.

Hugging me to him, Shane lays us down, spooning behind me, he reaches for the basket and pulls out another blanket and tosses it over us. We lay there until the sun is close to the horizon. Eventually Shane stirs, and sits up enough to grab the pie and a fork. We share the pie, finishing our beer, until the sun sets, and then, pulling on our clothes we ride back to the house. *This has been the most perfect evening of my life.*

Falling into bed together, we kiss and talk and eventually sleep. I wake up early, it's still dark out, but I don't know if Shane is ready to have Katie seeing me walk out in the morning, so I quietly pull on my clothes. Shane leans up on an elbow as I zip my jeans. Walking over to the bed, I kiss him softly.

"I'll see you later," I whisper.

"I love you," his voice is rough with sleep, his hand warm as he slides it up my hip. *This is it, he is it, he's my one.*

"I love you back," I whisper with a little smile.

What's in a Name?

N^{*ica*}

Wren is at my office bright and early Monday, anxious to hear all about Katie's weekend. Shane said that Katie was bubbling over all morning about how amazing and perfect everything was, and then she fell asleep for the rest of the day.

I've got Wren running all over the office, referencing numbers and pricing for me. Today I'm pitching the cosmetics line to my mother, and I want her to sign off on it without any strings attached. I want her support, but I want her to trust me enough to make it a profitable success on my own terms.

By noon I'm ready, and I'm planning to video conference with my parents this afternoon. I walk outside and sit in one of the chairs, relaxing and trying not to be nervous. I jump slightly and freeze when I feel something brush against my leg. Looking down, the scared little kitten that's been sleeping back here most nights is winding around my ankle.

I carefully reach a hand down under her belly, and when she doesn't panic, I lift her up carefully and look at her. She's a blend of colors, black with orange and yellow spots, a little bit of white, I'm assuming this is what calico looks like. Her gold eyes are watching me carefully, so I set her in my lap and stroke a finger between her ears. She sits still a moment and then kneads my thigh with her little claws, curls up and goes to sleep.

About a half hour later, even though I don't want to wake her, I gently set the sleepy kitten on the ground beside me and get up to head inside. To my surprise, she follows me right in as if she has lived here forever. I dig through the cupboards and manage to find a can of albacore tuna, I put a spoonful on a plate and she devours it. I put the rest in the fridge for later and head upstairs to change. The kitten hot on my heels.

As I get ready, I hold a one-sided conversation with my new pet, and quickly text Wren to pick up whatever things kittens need while she's out today. I'm sure Wren can show me all of that, she's a smart girl. *I'm going to be so sad to see her go in the fall.*

About ten minutes before the video call, Shane pulls up at the curb. He's got Chinese take out containers with him.

"Figured you probably didn't stop for lunch," he smiles, kissing me on his way to the kitchen.

"You figured right," I follow him out, scooping up the kitten on my way, "this is Peach, by the way," Shane smiles and holds out a finger for Peach to swat.

"She's a cute one, finally talked her in out of the yard huh?" He smiles, pushing one of the containers my way. We eat lunch in companionable silence and then I glance at the clock.

"I've got to video conference my mother about the new line

I'd like to spearhead, it's going to be kind of a big deal for me," I explain, "you can hang out if you want, or I can see you later?" He shakes his head.

"I'm not busy, I'll stick around for moral support," snagging my hand he brushes a kiss across my knuckles.

Twenty minutes later, Evelyn has said yes to everything I ask, and damn if she doesn't look proud.

"I have complete faith in you Veevee, you'll make this yours," she says warmly, "…and speaking of, what are you going to call your new venture?" I hesitate, I've thought about this, of course, but I'm still unsure until Shane speaks up.

"I think Nica Tyler Cosmetics has a nice ring to it," his voice is clear and steady. Shane walks around the table and when I turn to him, stunned, he drops to one knee. "That is, if I can get you to marry me." He holds out his hand and a diamond sparkles in the box he's holding. My hands fly up to my face as what he just said registers in my brain.

"Oh my god, yes, yes Shane, I will marry you!" He grabs me around the waist and swings me into his arms, kissing me hard, and then we break apart laughing as I hear my mother, sounding *very* un-Evelyn-like on the screen.

"Oh my god, John did you see that? I think Veronica just got engaged! I think she must be going by Nica now, we'll have to discuss that, look! Look John, VeeVee and Shane just got engaged!" Evelyn is tearful and smiling and seems to have completely forgotten that we can hear her. My father's face leans in and out of the frame, his arm around her shoulders.

"VeeVee darling, we'll talk soon, we love you," my father says quickly and ends the call.

Peach and a Parting

S hane

She said yes. That was a couple weeks ago, and the wedding planning is in full swing. Katie is over the moon, we're going to get married in the city with all Nica's people, and then throw another big reception here. I'm not sure Evelyn is ready to meet Wayne and Myrna yet.

Katie's play goes off like a dream, she steals the show. I hand Katie a bundle of daisies and then step back, smiling when Miles shyly offers her a dozen roses. *Smart kid.*

For the first time since I was a kid, the farm has a cat in the house. Peach is indoors and outdoors as she pleases, and she goes to work with Nica every morning.

I moved Nica to the farm, and the top floor of the building downtown is her new private office. She's hired on several new people, prepping for the day Wren leaves.

I know that Wren is thinking hard about staying, she loves

her job and she's learning so much from Nica about marketing and business. I pull up to the office with lunch packed up by Judy, and when I walk in the doors, I'm surprised to find Wren crying in Nica's arms. She sees me and mops her face and then gives Nica a hug.

"I've got to go call my gran," she stammers, sketching me a wave as she hurries out the door.

"What was that about?" I start pulling out the food, watching her face, it's a beautiful combination of happy and wistful.

"I'm sending her to college," Nica reaches for a sandwich, taking a bite absentmindedly, "she needs to go do her own thing, she needs to live her life. I told her there's always a place for her in my office if she wants to come back, but I think that girl's really going to be something, Shane," she looks at me with tears in her eyes, "I'm going to miss her something awful though." She's quiet for a moment, thinking.

"I hope she finds her way back to the country someday," she muses, "it's certainly been the best thing that ever happened to me."

* * *

Thanks for reading! If you enjoyed Veronica's story, here's a hint of what comes next for her assistant Wren.

Finding My Safe

~~~~~~~~~~

Wren

Bachelorette parties suck. Elbowing my way through the crowded bar, I curse Gran for teaching me manners as a child. If it weren't for her, I would have given this whole night a hard pass. Instead, here I am, getting another round of shots for Jenna and her friends who can, at best, be called acquaintances from med school. Squeezing between a rock and a hard place; in the form of a man so firmly wedged onto his stool that I question if he died a few days ago and a trucker with a sun-dried tomato for a face who sighs and moves ever so slightly, I wave at the bartender and glance around.

You know that no-man's land where the country meets the city? You're driving through street lights and neighborhoods and BAM, nothing for about a mile before the fields and barns start? That's where Joe's Bar sits, right smack in the middle of that city-country deadzone. It's a pretty average crappy bar, full of hard-drinking regulars, the occasional hipsters who roll in looking for an experience, bar flies who reek of cheap perfume and desperation, and a party of silly girls hogging up the tiny dance floor. *That's me. I'm with the silly girls.*

Waving at the bartender again, I walk myself back through the conversation that brought me to this point. Jenna approached me earlier today with the friendliest smile I'd ever seen on her face. *There's the mistake...I fell for that crocodile smile.* She fed me some kind of sob story about Monica not having many local friends who would throw her a hen party, *boo-freakin-hoo, I fell for that too.* Yep, and now here I am, buying a round, for these silly drunks I barely know. *I should bail.*

"Hurry up Wren!! We're sooooo thirsty!" Monica trills, dancing in a circle with her stupid plastic champagne glass held high. She's gaining the attention of the pool players nearby. Pausing their game to look at her, the nearest one grins at his friends and loops an arm around her waist as she dances by, pulling her in tight. *Oh great, this could get bad fast.* I'm too far away to hear what he's saying, but her smile quickly fades and she starts squirming free, so it's not hard to guess at his intentions.

Jenna stomps over, finger raised in a very official angry point to give him a piece of her mind, but one of his buddies twirls her into his arms, laughing rudely as she squeals indignantly. I glance at the bartender who gives a decidedly overworked sigh. Picking up his phone from under the bar, he appears to check the time before tossing the phone on the counter and continuing to pour drinks.

"Thanks bud, you're a big help," I grumble as I shove away from the bar and make my way back through the crowd. I can see angry tears brimming in Monica's eyes as she swats away the offending hands of the dipshit who won't leave her alone. *See now, that's not fair...and this is her hen party damnit...* Pasting a smile on my face I put a little bounce in my step, *all the better to get close to you losers.* The two men who are bothering the girls see me coming and glance at each other before smiling at me.

"Well good evening Sugar," the one bothering Monica lets go of her waist, tipping an invisible hat at me, his voice oily as his eyes scan me top to tail. It doesn't take him long, I'm five foot nothing, and I walk right up close while he gets an eye-full. Not wasting a beat, I get in his space, grab his nuts, and squeeze. Hard. As his smile quickly turns to an open-mouthed bellow of pain, he curls in on himself trying to get away from me. I help the momentum along, pushing his head straight down on the edge of the pool table with a satisfying thunk and he falls to the floor, dazed, holding his squished nuts. *Just like you taught me Gran.*

"What the hell?!" His buddy lets Jenna loose and looks back and forth from his fallen friend to me several times in rapid succession. *Now to get us out of this mess.*

"You stupid jackasses," I fill my normally sweet Southern voice with as much disdain as I can drum up. "Do you know who these girls' Daddies are?" I point at Jenna, Monica and Courtney, "CEO, Senator, Sheriff, and you think you can just paw their *baby girls*?" Idiot number one is still on the floor, but his buddies are backing away looking seriously uncomfortable.

I shake my head in disgust. "Apologize and get back to your game, you hear?" They mumble 'sorry' and turn back to the pool table shame-faced, but the idiot on the floor isn't quite ready to give up.

"Whatever bitch," he groans, climbing painfully to his feet, eyes narrowed. *Damnit.*

Turning to the girls, I decide to herd them to the door and find a bouncer to walk us to our car. A hard poke in the shoulder turns me back to the angry idiot with sore nuts.

"We ain't done yet sweetie," he leers, confidence returning, as he reaches out a finger to twirl a strand of my blonde hair. I swat him away, angry. As I'm deciding whether to dust off a few more tricks Gran taught me or just insist that the bartender get off his ass and call the cops or something, Sore Nuts jerks his hand away like he touched a hot stove.

"My apologies, we thought you girls wanted to dance. We're just going to play pool now and leave you be." His words tumble out in a rush, fear in his eyes as he stares over my head. *The hell?*

"Hey Kane, didn't know you were working tonight," Sore Nuts continues, trying to sound calm. *Kane? Ohmygod.* I whirl around and almost bash my nose into a very hard chest covered in a flannel work shirt. Taking a tiny step back I look up and see a grim face I'd recognize anywhere. He doesn't glance at me as he gives Sore Nuts a hard look.

"Roy, Charlie," he rumbles, looking at each of them in turn. "Looks like your game is over." He sets his jaw, I can see the muscles working under his beard. It's shorter than I remember it, he used to keep it long, now it's just barely long enough to grab. *That's not a weird measurement at all, where did that come from, wow.* Darker red, almost brown, as if he's not in the sun as much as he used to be when he worked on the farm. *His hair used to be such a golden red, I always thought he looked like a lion. I wonder if he remembers me.*

"Yeahhhh, I got an early shift tomorrow," Roy's voice startles me and I turn and watch as he stretches his arms overhead and gives a fake yawn, "better call it." Trying to save face, Charlie nods and they head for the door. The men they were with don't

153

even glance my way as they return to their pool game. I turn back to Kane and he looks down at me, recognition sparking in his eyes.

It's been almost four years since I last saw him, but I'd know those eyes anywhere. Hazel with green and blue flecks, he's got light lashes, thick and long. Almost pretty if the rest of him weren't so *man*. I don't know how tall he is, but I'm staring him in the sternum, so he's way over 6'. Thick muscles roll under the work shirt, wide neck, broad shoulders, he's built like a bull but he moves like a fighter. My grandad would've had eyes on him in a minute, ready to get him in the ring.

"Hi Kane, it's been a while." I realize we haven't said anything yet and the words whisper out. The tiniest smile edges up the corner of his mouth.

"Wren." He's always quiet, no extra words needed, so I'm actually a little surprised when he continues, "You're a long way from Gravity."

"So are you," I counter, "no one knew where you went, you just up and left..." trailing off, I don't know what else to say. I'd known him because Gravity was a small town. I'd been dating a guy he worked with and met him just once. The next day, Kane was gone. *Leaving me memories of a dance, the feel of his lips pressing into my hair, and a slightly-confused broken heart.*

"Yeah, um...Mike with you?" He shifts his shoulders uncomfortably and glances around as I blurt out a little laugh.

"That's a no, he figured out I was actually going to go to college and knocked up Ella Harkins before my end of the truck seat was cold." It doesn't even hurt, I haven't thought about Mike in a long time.

"Sorry," Kane frowns, like I'm going to cry or something, and I laugh again.

"Nothing to be sorry for, Mike is a memory at this point, he was fun to date right after high school while I was taking classes and saving." I toss my hair back over my shoulder and decide to try again. "So why did you leave Gravity without sayin' a word?"

"So med school?" His voice cuts across mine, throwing me off. At the same time Jenna's voice drowns us both out.

"Oh my god Wren you were so cave-girl with that guy! That was in-*sane*! I'm totally pissed I didn't get a clip of that to post!" Her lip pouts out and while she takes a breath she gives Kane an eye-banging and bumps her shoulder into mine. "Aren't you going to introduce me?" *No, I don't want to and get your eyes back in your fool head, Jenna.*

"Jenna, Kane. Kane, Jenna." I try to keep my voice friendly and barely succeed. A happy little butterfly herd fills my chest when his eyes barely flick her way. He gives her a nod and ignores her outstretched hand. Leaning down, his mouth close enough to my ear that I feel his breath tickling my skin, I can hear the smile he's hiding.

"It was good to see you Wren, I'm sorry I didn't say goodbye." He doesn't glance at either of us again as he turns and shoulders his way through the crowd, leaving us staring at his back.

"What a dick." Jenna sniffs, turning away. I nod bemusedly and follow her back to the dance floor.

About the Author

Halo Roberts is a writer of steamy rom-coms, lover of coffee and dark beer, and spoiler of two fat cats affectionately known as the Bitchy Betas. She's living happily ever after in Iowa with her very own hunky farm boy, and a small herd of stubborn mules that look a lot like children.

Head on over to haloroberts.com, sign up for Halo's newsletter and receive a free download of her short story, A Night at the Diner.

You can connect with me on:

- http://haloroberts.com
- https://twitter.com/RobertsHalo
- https://www.facebook.com/halorobertsauthor
- https://www.bookbub.com/profile/halo-roberts
- https://www.instagram.com/halorobertswrites
- http://bit.ly/halogoodreads

Subscribe to my newsletter:

✉ http://haloroberts.com

Also by Halo Roberts

Sweet, steamy, laugh-out-loud romantic comedies that always end in a happily ever after…or two.

Finding My Night
Second star to the right...

A sassy chef with a crush on her boss finds herself on a 'not-a-date' with him in this hilariously steamy romp. Complete with a problematic socialite, a cream puff fiasco, and a killer dress with a strategic peek of lace, there might also be a man-bun…a pair of dueling best friends…and a wedding…or two.

Finding My One
Blue skies and dirt roads and peaches, oh my...

A real job with the family business or goodbye trust fund...my parents have lost their minds. The icing on this craptastic cake is setting up headquarters in some backwater southern town, complete with a partner...a rugged, country, single dad that flips every switch I've got...and a few I didn't know about. ~Veronica

Things are heating up in the country...

Finding My Safe
The songs say love is in the water... and strange...

When chance brings Wren and Kane together again, things have changed. Wren is graduating med school, soon to start her residency. Kane is a bouncer at a crappy roadside bar. When an ambush in an alley makes him depend on Wren far more than he expected, can they find love in the midst of five-dollar tequila shots, surprise proposals and the bright lights of Las Vegas?

Here's hoping love is also at Joe's bar...and not actually strange.

Finding My Sun

Breakups suck.

They suck even more after you drunkenly tell your A-list rock star boyfriend that you love him…then find your now ex best friend in his bed. Welcome to Laurel's world. So, what's a girl with a mangled heart to do? Escape to the Caribbean for some sun, sangria, and…a surfer?

Laurel meets Trey and sparks fly, hammocks flip, and all signs point to love. But when best friend and rock star drama invades the island, can new love last? Laurel has decisions to make, hearts to break and a sunburn to avoid in this two-part romantic comedy.